# Jade and the Stray

**The Pony Tales series**

1. Jade and the Stray

*Coming soon . . .*

2. Jade at the Champs

# Jade and the Stray

## AMY BROWN

HarperCollins*Publishers*

**HarperCollins***Publishers*
First published 2010
HarperCollins*Publishers (New Zealand) Limited*
P.O. Box 1, Auckland 1140

Copyright © Amy Brown 2010

**HarperCollins***Publishers*
31 View Road, Glenfield, Auckland 0627, New Zealand
25 Ryde Road, Pymble, Sydney, NSW 2073, Australia
A 53, Sector 57, Noida, UP, India
77–85 Fulham Palace Road, London W6 8JB, United Kingdom
2 Bloor Street East, 20th floor, Toronto, Ontario M4W 1A8, Canada
10 East 53rd Street, New York, NY 10022, USA

National Library of New Zealand Cataloguing-in-Publication Data

Brown, Amy, 1984-
Jade and the stray / Amy Brown.
(Pony tales)
ISBN 978-1-86950-842-5
1. Horses—Juvenile fiction. [1.Horses—Fiction.] I. Title.
II. Series: Brown, Amy, 1984- Pony tales.
NZ823.3—dc 22

ISBN: 978 1 86950 842 5
Cover design by Ingrid Kwong
Cover photography by Steve Baccon
Special thanks to the Malabar Riding School
Typesetting by Springfield West

Printed by Griffin Press, Australia
50 gsm Bulky News used by HarperCollins*Publishers* is a natural,
recyclable product made from wood grown in sustainable
plantation forests. The manufacturing processes conform to the
environmental regulations in the country of origin, New Zealand.

# Who are you?

Since leaving Rose and her mum at the bus station in Auckland, Jade had driven through many small towns, counting horses to keep her mind off things. Some towns had giant corrugated-iron sheep and statues of dogs, others not much more than a local pub and a dairy. Flaxton seemed like the latter. First there were scrubby paddocks and pine trees, then the main street with a few boring shops — the Salvation Army, a café and an old ladies' clothes store. Jade felt like crying again. How could she live here after Auckland?

As the bus pulled into a small car park, Jade saw her granddad sitting in his old white Falcon. He was reading a newspaper and smoking a cigarette. She also saw a group of girls about her age walk past, towards the KFC. They were different — different from Rose and the other girls at Jade's school in Auckland. Their clothes were different, their faces and laughs were different.

When the driver passed her the suitcase she'd packed herself, Jade wanted to hop straight back on the bus. Why couldn't she live with Rose's family? She hardly knew her granddad. They only ever met at Christmas. The Christmas before last they'd all been there — her mum, dad and grandma. And now it was just her left.

'Hello, Jade.' Her granddad was behind her now, reaching for her suitcase. She gave it to him as they hugged awkwardly, sort of patting each other's backs. 'How're you doing?'

'All right.' Jade hadn't seen him since the funeral. He was wearing an old checked shirt, stained jeans and work boots now, which suited him. He fitted in here, as she did in Auckland. He smelt of petrol. Jade wondered if she'd ever get used to that smell.

They drove to her granddad's house without having to talk — Jade looking out the window and her granddad listening to Dolly Parton.

'That's your new school,' he said as they passed a concrete gateway and a set of ugly yellow buildings. Jade didn't have anything nice to say, so she said nothing.

As they pulled into Grove Road, the view became more familiar. Over a bridge, there was the farm animal pound — a place for stray goats, sheep, cattle and horses. Jade wound down the window as they passed it, to get a better look at a big black pony with four white stockings. It stopped grazing and watched her blowing a raspberry, trying to whiffle like a horse. Her granddad smirked.

'You still like horses?' he asked.

'Yeah.'

'Thought you might've grown out of that.'

'Nah.'

'Plenty of horses round here. Mind you, don't get too attached. It won't be there forever.'

'What happens to the strays that aren't collected?' Jade knew what her granddad meant, but wanted him to say it.

'They get dog-tuckered.'

'Put down?'

'Well, they go to the abattoir.' As her granddad said this he rolled down his window and spat. He clearly wasn't used to being around eleven-year-old girls.

Shortly, they drew up outside the battered old bungalow. Jade knew which room to go to, as she'd stayed there before a couple of years ago, and nothing had changed since. Perhaps it was dustier now, without her grandma's cleaning, but otherwise everything was as she'd left it. There was still a pile of Golden Books sitting on the dresser — they'd been too young for her then, and were even less appropriate now.

From her window, she had a view out over the backyard. The lawn was grey and tufty — too dry to bother mowing. The garden had got away on her granddad.

Jade was just glad she didn't have to look at all

the bits of cars out the front in the garage. Lennox's Auto Repairs was her granddad's business and it didn't interest her one bit.

She was quick to unpack her things. Jeans and T-shirts, folded more clumsily than when her mum used to do it, went in the chest of drawers next to the window. The dress from last year's school social, which was already getting too small, and the black waistcoat that she'd worn to the funeral went in the wardrobe. Jade's faded toy rabbit sat awkwardly on the pillow, and her five favourite books were piled on the bedside table. Rose's mum was posting her other stuff down soon, but for now she had to make do with what she had.

The familiar smell of her clothes was overwhelmed by the stale old-person scent that filled the house. Everything looked and smelt pale brown, like tobacco, old curtains and old carpet. *I'm the only young thing in this room,* Jade thought.

She lay on the bed and opened one of her books — *International Velvet*. She didn't have to start at the beginning, she'd read it so many times before. She could hear her mum's voice reading to her, stopping at intervals to say, 'Really, Jade, this is awful! How can you enjoy it?'

'Because it's got horses,' Jade remembered replying. Her mum had argued that there were probably better stories with horses that she could read: *National Velvet* for instance, or *Fly-by-Night*, or *My Friend Flicka*. Those three sat on Jade's bedside table now, along with *Jill's Gymkhana*, *Pony Club Cup* and *The Black Stallion*. Why had she only brought her babyish horse stories? She felt both silly and relieved. She knew she was getting too old for them, but only these books could help her get to sleep at night. There's nothing like a story about a beautiful, clever horse and a young rider to take your mind off real troubles. Jade was trying hard not to think about her dad.

After finishing *International Velvet* for the umpteenth time, Jade looked at her watch and saw that it was nearly six. She remembered that her granddad liked to eat early and thought she'd better go out and be sociable. She could smell something boiling.

'Hello, Jade,' her granddad said as she came into the kitchen. He was bent over the oven, turning something over in a dish. Grandma had always cooked; Jade wondered what Granddad's dinner would be like.

'Shall I set the table?' Jade asked.

'Ah, yes,' Granddad said unsurely. 'It should be ready quite soon, I think.'

Jade found the place mats with native birds painted on them in the sideboard drawer, and cutlery in the kitchen. Last time she was here, her grandma had fussed over the state of the cloth napkins. Jade didn't think her granddad would mind if they didn't use them tonight.

When she'd finished setting the table, Jade sat down in her usual chair and looked around at the empty seats. *This isn't doing me any good*, she thought, and went back into the kitchen.

'Can I help with anything, Granddad?'

'How are you at mashing spuds?' he asked, not

looking up from a steamy pot on top of the oven.

Jade had never mashed potatoes before; it was her dad's job. 'I'm OK at it,' she said hopefully. 'Where's the masher?'

'You'll find it in the drawer to your left.'

Over her eleven years Jade had eaten better dinners, but when she'd finished and put her knife and fork together she told her granddad it was good.

'You like roast pork, then?' he said.

'Yeah, it was nice, thanks.'

'Not bad for a first go, I reckon.' He sounded surprised and pleased with himself. 'Now for the dishes.'

'Granddad?' Jade asked, after she'd finished drying their few dishes.

'Yes?'

'Do you mind if I go for a quick walk?'

'No, that should be all right.' Again, he seemed unsure. 'Where do you think you'll go?'

'Just down the road a bit.' Jade wanted to say hello to the pony with the four white stockings.

'Want me to come with you?'

'Nah, I'll be fine. Call the police if I'm not back in half an hour.'

'Right you are.'

As Jade put on her shoes outside the fly-screen door, she heard her granddad opening a beer and turning on the TV.

It was a lovely summer evening — still light and warm at seven o'clock. Jade walked along the grass verge, unaccustomed to so much space without any people around. As she approached the paddock of stray animals, she started looking for good grass. Most of it was coarse and dry, but down by a culvert she found a few handfuls of lush clover.

Jade called the pony, clicking her tongue against the roof of her mouth. 'Come on, boy, this clover's for you.'

She held it out over the fence and called again. Eventually the pony looked up at her and pricked his ears. He started ambling over, but too slowly. A scrawny ginger-coloured goat had seen Jade's handful of greenery and galloped towards it, making a terrible noise.

'Oi, this isn't for you!' Jade laughed, pushing the goat's head away as its little hooves scrabbled to stand on the bottom wire of the fence.

'Maaaa!' the goat whined, its yellow eyes looking pathetic and hungry. Jade gave in and fed the goat a small handful of grass.

'Don't worry, mister — the rest is for you.' The pony had arrived by now and stuck his nose over the fence and into the palm of her hand.

'You're in a bit of a state, aren't you, my dear,' Jade told the pony, stroking his thin neck and trying to comb his tangled mane with her fingers. As she started scratching his eyebrow, the pony cocked his head to one side, closed his eyes and made a blissful snickering sound.

'Like that, do you?' Jade laughed. The goat, bored when it wasn't being fed, left the pony and Jade alone together.

'I reckon you'd scrub up nicely,' Jade told the pony. 'You're quite tall, aren't you?'

'She's actually talking to a horse!' a mean voice

said. Jade spun around in a fright: three girls on roller-blades were hovering behind her.

'Hi,' Jade said coldly. She could tell she wouldn't be making any friends here.

'Who are you?' the ringleader asked. She had three studs in each ear and bleached hair. She looked about thirteen, as did her scowling friends.

'I'm Jade.'

'Everyone,' the ringleader said to her girlfriends, 'this is Jade. She's in love with a horse.' The girls started screeching with laughter. 'Do you like horses more than boys, Jade?'

Not seeing any reason why she should lie, Jade said, 'Yes, actually. Horses are great. They're way smarter than most boys — and you, by the looks of it.'

The ringleader reeled back. Clearly, she was used to getting the last word.

'Enjoy your horsey boyfriend while you can, eh? You know what's going to happen to him, don't you?'

Jade didn't bother replying; she just turned around and started stroking her friend's neck again.

'He's gonna get made into glue and dog food soon!' The ringleader made her friends laugh like hyenas as they all roller-bladed away.

'Mate, you're not going to get made into glue while I'm around,' Jade whispered to the pony. 'Meet me at the gate in a few hours.'

Back at the house, Jade's granddad was watching *Coronation Street*. She'd thought only her grandma had liked it, and could have sworn that her grand-dad usually grumbled through it.

'Nice walk?' he asked as she passed the living-room door.

'Yes, thanks.'

'Did you go down to visit that pony?'

For some reason Jade was embarrassed at this. 'Yeah.'

'You off to bed now, then?'

'Um, I might have a shower first. Is that OK?'

'Towels are in the hall cupboard. Good night, Jade.'

'OK. Thanks. Good night.'

It was like staying in an awkward hotel. Was Jade expected to kiss her granddad good night, as she would have her mum or dad? She hoped not, and ran down to her room to get her pyjamas.

Warm from her shower, Jade sat tensely on the edge of the bed, waiting for her granddad's light to go out. It was only nine and not completely dark yet. A moth fluttered against the lampshade above Jade's bed. She lay back again and decided to read a few chapters of *The Black Stallion*.

Before she knew it, Alec the young jockey was racing the black stallion around the track for the first time and her watch said eleven-thirty. Jade peered out into the hallway and saw that her granddad's light was finally off; she could even hear him snoring.

Quickly, she changed back into her shorts and T-shirt, laced up her shoes and left the house, being careful not to slam the door. It was shadowy around her granddad's garage as Jade looked for some rope. *Why didn't I do this when it was light?*

she scolded herself. Eventually, finding the light switch by the door, Jade saw three coils of rope hanging against the far wall. She walked carefully across the concrete floor stained with grease, and grabbed the smallest coil.

'Yes, that'll do fine,' she said to herself in a singsong voice as she turned the light switch off and found herself in the dark.

In the dark it seemed like a long way back to the strays' paddock. Once a hedgehog scuttled across the road in front of her and Jade gasped. *Don't be a silly baby*, she told herself under her breath.

At the paddock, all she could see of the pony was his four white stockings. She called him as she had before, and this time he came trotting over.

'Hello, lovely,' she said, knotting the rope as best she could through the ring in the pony's old halter. The rest of the animals must have been sleeping, because no goat or sheep tried to squeeze through the gate as Jade fiddled with the rusty latch.

'Lucky it wasn't locked, eh?' she said to the

pony, stroking his neck and shoulder with the palm of her hand.

Leading him down the shadowy grass verge, Jade started to worry. She could feel the pony's tense body through the rope. Getting out of the paddock was exciting for the pony, but did he trust her? Should he trust her?

'Oh, no! Where am I going to put you when we get back to Granddad's?'

Stopping to think her plan through, Jade let the hungry pony tear at the lush grass growing at the bottom of the culvert. There wouldn't be grass like that on her granddad's back lawn, that was for sure. The verge outside the front gate was a bit greener, but the pony mightn't be safe out there. Jade thought of the girls with the roller-blades.

'Perhaps I should just put you back, fella?' Jade said to the pony, frowning. It was a silly plan, but she'd set her heart on it now and didn't want to give up.

'Nope. You're coming with me. We'll sort something out.'

# Mr White's idea

Early the next morning when Jade's granddad started making his breakfast, he looked out the kitchen window and saw his granddaughter lying asleep on the back lawn with a familiar black pony grazing calmly next to her.

'Good heavens!' he said to himself. 'That naughty girl!'

When Jade woke up, she was cold and stiff, and had forgotten where she was. The first thing she noticed was her granddad standing over her with a frown on his face. The next thing she noticed was a pair of legs with white stockings standing near her head, and a black nose rubbing hopefully at the grey lawn.

'Sorry, Granddad,' she said.

'What were you thinking, girl?'

'I didn't want him to get made into glue.' Jade had picked herself up off the ground now and was brushing grass off her shorts.

'We can't keep a horse, Jade. There's no room. Surely you can see that?'

'Yeah.' For a horrible moment, Jade thought she was going to start crying, but she swallowed and continued, 'I guess I should just take him back and hope someone else saves him.'

'I think so, yes.' Her granddad patted her shoulder and then stroked the pony's neck. 'He's a quiet fellow, isn't he? Didn't stand on you during the night?'

Jade looked at her granddad; he was smiling slightly now. She started laughing. 'Nope, not once.'

Before taking the pony back to the strays' paddock, Jade, at her granddad's insistence, had some
toast and Milo. She was unusually hungry and
was just spreading apricot jam on her fourth piece
of toast, when a ute and horse-float pulled in the
driveway.

'Granddad, there's someone here.'

'That'll be Jim. He said he'd be round early.'

When she'd finished her toast and rinsed her
plate, Jade went out to see the pony.

'Sorry, fella,' she said. 'Got to take you back
to the pound; nothing for you to eat here.' The
pony quickly proved her wrong by starting to strip
leaves off her granddad's pittosporum hedge.

'Oh, you want to stay, don't you?' Jade sighed,
resting her head on the pony's neck.

'You shouldn't let her eat that,' a voice said. Jade
turned around and saw a tall, bald man wearing a
homespun jersey. 'It's poisonous for horses.'

Jade quickly pulled on the lead rope and yanked
the pony's head away from the hedge. 'Is it a she?'
Jade asked the man, surprised. 'I'd thought it was
a stallion.'

The man laughed. 'No, she's definitely a mare. With feeding and riding she could be a lovely pony — a bit ewe-necked, but kind eyes. What do you call her? Not Bob or Derek, I hope.'

'She doesn't have a name — she isn't mine.' Jade looked guiltily at the man, wondering what 'ewe-necked' meant.

'Oh,' he said.

'I stole her from the pound last night because I didn't want her to get made into glue, but we haven't got enough room or grass for her here, so I have to take her back now.' This spilled out of Jade's mouth before she knew what she was saying. To her relief, the man didn't look disappointed or start laughing at her. He smiled, but his expression was serious.

'That's a shame. But you're absolutely right, there's not enough space here for her. In fact, if she'd been yours, I would've offered you grazing at my place.'

Jade's face lit up. 'Really?'

'Yes. If it doesn't work out with the mare, you're welcome to visit my horses. Well, one of them is my daughter's really, but she's gone to university now, so they're not getting much riding.'

Jade was barely listening; all she could think about was the offer of grazing for the stray.

'Granddad?' she called, running around to the driveway where he was fixing the tail-light on the horse-float. 'Granddad!'

'What's all this caterwauling about, girl?' he yelled back. 'Come and talk to me properly.' Jade left the tall man with the mare and ran over.

'Granddad, the man has a paddock with horses and there's enough room there for my pony, the stray, if I'm allowed to keep her — I thought it was a he, but it's a she — I'd probably be allowed to keep her, wouldn't I, if I had grazing?' The words just tumbled out. 'Granddad, can I keep her? Please!' Jade pleaded.

Jade hadn't been this happy since the accident, and Granddad was delighted to see it.

'Jade, love, it's not as simple as that. I hate to say it, but you've taken that pony without asking. It's not yours. And even if it were, there's more to owning a pony than having somewhere to keep it.

How would you pay Mr White for grazing?'

Mr White had come over to the float too, now, and was looking a bit embarrassed. 'Look, Ed, if Jade here — it is Jade, isn't it? — if Jade wants to keep this mare and is willing to work hard to get her into good condition, then I'm happy to help. Payment won't be necessary. Though, Jade,' Mr White looked at her seriously now, 'if the pound lets you keep the mare, can you promise me that she'll be your greatest responsibility?'

'Yes,' Jade said, as thoughtfully as she could.

'Do you know much about keeping a horse?' Mr White asked kindly.

'Um, I guess not. But I know it's a lot of work and that's fine — I don't mind hard work. I'm a fast learner, too.' Jade didn't usually talk herself up, but she could tell this was the moment to do it.

Mr White smiled. 'Well, best of luck with the pound. If it's good news, give me a call and I'll pop back around with the float.'

'This is very good of you, Jim,' Jade's granddad said to Mr White as he hopped into his ute. 'There won't be a bill for the light.'

'It's a pleasure,' Mr White said, looking at Jade too. 'Since Abby left home I haven't been spending enough time with the horses, other than feeding them and cleaning the paddock. It'll be nice to have an excuse to get back out there.'

As Mr White drove out, Jade asked her grand-dad, 'Cleaning the paddock? What did he mean by that?'

Her granddad chortled. 'Picking up the, er, manure, I think. You'd be up to that, would you?'

'Anything to keep her,' Jade said, grinning and flinging her arms around the patient pony's neck.

The rest of the morning was spent talking on the phone to the pound, and then waiting for one of their representatives to come over. Not surprisingly, the woman on the phone was none too pleased to hear Jade admit to stealing a horse from their paddock. But the younger woman who arrived just after lunch, Olivia, saw the funny side.

'I remember when I was young I thought about

doing that. I shouldn't say this, but I'm impressed that you actually went through with it.'

'She stayed out all night, sleeping on the lawn next to the pony,' Granddad said, almost proudly.

'Well, I can see that you love her,' Olivia said to Jade, who was holding onto the stray's mane. 'But this is no place for a pony, as I think you know.'

'Yeah, I know. I told the lady on the phone that we had somewhere better to put her,' Jade interrupted.

'Hold on, I was getting to that. What I heard from your phone conversation is that Jim White has offered to graze this pony. Is that true?'

'Yes, it is,' Granddad cut in.

'Well, in that case, I think she's in safe hands. I know Jim — I was a friend of his daughter — and I know that he'll teach you how to care for a horse.'

'Thank you so much! That's so cool!' Jade said, forgetting she was trying to sound grown-up.

The young woman from the pound laughed. 'I'm glad you're pleased. Just make sure you don't prove me wrong. I'll be very disappointed if in a few months I hear that Jim has an unwanted horse abandoned on his property.'

'She's definitely not unwanted, I promise.'

And so the stray was now no longer a stray, and Jade wasted no time in calling Mr White and arranging for the pony to be moved to her new home.

'Remember that he's doing you a favour — don't be too pushy,' Jade's granddad told her, after she'd hung up the phone.

'I don't mean to be pushy, I'm just excited. I'm so glad that the pony's going to a nice home. I can't believe she's mine, Granddad!' Jade's smile was so radiant that her granddad, though tempted, couldn't bring himself to remind her of all the hard work ahead — and that school was due to start in four days. It was so good to see her genuinely happy. He'd wait until dinner time to discuss serious matters.

Mr White arrived at quarter to four with his horse-float. When he got out of the ute, he was carrying a long rope with a loop at one end.

'What's that?' Jade asked, as she led her new pony over to the float.

'I call it a "bum-rope",' Mr White said. 'It may be that madam here,' he continued, patting the pony's neck gently, 'hasn't travelled by float for a while. If she doesn't want to walk up the ramp, we'll throw this loop here around her rump and thread the end here through the ring of her halter, like so.' He effortlessly demonstrated. 'Now,' he said, 'if she's reluctant, we can give the rope a little tug and she'll feel some pressure on her behind, which should make her keep walking. Doesn't look like we'll need it, though,' Mr White said, smiling. 'She seems rather relaxed.'

Jade held her pony's lead rope and the long end of the bum-rope, while Mr White lowered the ramp of the horse-float. Inside, there was a clean rubber mat to stop the horses' hooves slipping and a hay-net full of fragrant lucerne hay. As Mr White had predicted, Jade's new pony needed no encouragement to walk up the ramp. As soon as she saw and smelt the hay, she headed up of her own accord, dragging Jade with her.

'She loves it in here,' Jade laughed, patting her pony's neck and watching her whiskery lips taking great mouthfuls of hay.

'I reckon she's a bit hungry after her stint at the pound,' Mr White said, deftly tying the lead rope in a slipknot to a loop of twine next to the hay-net and then unthreading the bum-rope. Jade's heart sank a little as she watched this, realizing fully for the first time how little she knew about keeping horses.

When the ramp was up and Jade had said goodbye to her granddad, she jumped into the passenger seat of Mr White's ute and drove away to greener pastures.

Dusty Springfield was playing on the tape deck.

'My mum used to listen to this,' Jade told Mr White quietly.

'It's a good album.' Mr White didn't seem like he was going to ask about the accident, and Jade was relieved, sort of. Strangely, it almost made her want him to ask how she was feeling. Perhaps he didn't know what had happened. Jade looked at his weathered face staring straight at the road and reckoned that he probably did know; it looked like a knowledgeable face.

Soon they pulled into a limestone driveway lined with beech trees. Mr White parked the float between a paddock with post-and-rail fenced yards and a huge corrugated-iron garage.

Far down the paddock, Jade could see two big horses grazing together. They lifted their heads and pricked their ears as the new pony backed down the ramp and whinnied at them.

'These are your new friends, girl,' Jade told her, struggling to keep hold of the lead rope as the pony strained towards the paddock gate. 'She's really strong,' Jade said nervously, hoping Mr White would help.

'She's excited by her new surroundings,' he said, taking the lead rope and leaning into the pony's shoulder as he manoeuvred her through the gateway and into one of the yards. 'Were there any other horses in the pound with her?' he asked Jade as he untied the knotted lead rope and let the pony trot around the yard in her halter.

'No, just sheep and goats. She must've missed having horsey company.'

'It looks like it. I was going to teach you how to groom her today, but she's looking a bit too excitable at the moment. It might be best for her to let off some steam and meet Brandy and Hamlet this afternoon.'

'Are they Abby's horses?' Jade asked.

'Well, Hamlet's mine and Brandy is Abby's. Though she doesn't get to ride her much these days, unfortunately, since she went to university.'

'They have nice names,' Jade said. 'I don't know what to call my pony . . .'

'What about Pippi?' Mr White asked. 'As in Pippi Longstocking — it'd suit her white stockings.'

'I quite like that,' Jade said. 'But, maybe just Pip would be better?'

'Pip's a very good name for a stray,' Mr White said. 'She's a bit like Pip from *Great Expectations*.' Jade looked blankly at Mr White. 'You know,' he said, '*Great Expectations* by Charles Dickens?'

'I've heard of it,' Jade said vaguely, feeling out of

her depth again. 'Is Pip OK?' she asked, watching the pony frantically circling the yard.

'Just excited. We may as well let her out now — the other two are in the back paddock, so she can hoon around the front here without getting into trouble. It'll do her good.' Mr White carefully opened the yard gate and Pip raced out, bucking and pig-rooting before cantering down to the fence line where Brandy and Hamlet were waiting to meet her.

'She's been so calm until now,' Jade said. 'I didn't know she could go that fast.'

'Don't worry, she'll settle down soon,' Mr White said. He looked at his watch, 'It's nearly five — will your granddad expect you home soon?'

'I don't think so,' Jade said. 'But if Pip's busy running around, I may as well go home.'

'I was thinking it might be worth familiarizing you with the tack and grooming tools you'll be using tomorrow. It'll only take ten minutes.'

'Oh, yes please!' Jade was excited as Mr White rolled up the door of the shed and brought out a saddle, a bridle and a grooming kit. As he showed her how the girth buckled up and explained about the snaffle bit on the bridle, Jade's head began to swim. She tried to listen as carefully as she could, but there was just too much information to absorb at once.

'And there'll be a test tomorrow,' Mr White said, laughing at Jade's worried expression.

'Was all this stuff your daughter's?' Jade asked.

'Yep, we've had it since she rode ponies. It's good that you've come along, otherwise it'd go to waste.' Jade smiled at this, but still felt uncomfortable.

'I reckon Granddad is probably wondering where I am,' Jade said, looking across the paddock to where Pip and the Whites' horses were sniffing at each other. 'Look, she has calmed down now,' Jade said, relieved.

'She'll be fine,' Mr White said. 'Hello, dear!'

Jade looked around and saw a small silver-haired woman approaching. 'This is my wife, Ellen,' Mr White said to Jade. 'Ellen, this is Ed Lennox's granddaughter, Jade, whom I was telling you about. And that,' he said, pointing out into the paddock, 'is Pip.'

'Hi, Jade,' Mrs White said pleasantly. 'What a nice-looking animal you've got there. And it's good to see Abby's pony gear is finally getting some use. I was just thinking, Jade, do you have a helmet or riding boots?'

Jade blushed. 'No, but I've got jeans and sneakers.' She didn't want to seem like a charity case.

'You're about the same size that Abby was when she was your age — if you like, you could take some of her hand-me-downs.'

'Thanks heaps,' Jade said, embarrassed. 'That's really kind of you, Mrs White.'

'Good! Would you like to try them on now?'

This was too much for Jade. It was enough just seeing the Whites' beautiful paddocks and spare riding gear — to go into their house and try on their daughter's clothes made her feel exhausted. 'Perhaps, if it's OK, I could look at them tomorrow?' Jade said quietly. 'I should go home to Granddad now.' She hated how quiet her voice went when she was trying to sound polite.

'Of course, Jade. You're welcome to come over

tomorrow. If it's OK with your granddad, you could stay for lunch.'

'I'll ask. Thanks.'

'Now, shall I drop you home?' Mr White un-hooked the float from the ute while Jade clumsily carried the saddle and bridle back into the shed.

When she got home, Jade's granddad was in the kitchen, dishing out a casserole and boiled potatoes.

'Just in time for tea,' he said.

Jade was starving and ate quickly, mopping up the gravy with her potatoes and shovelling peas into her mouth.

'Slow down, girl. You'll choke if you don't chew.'

Jade smiled and slowed down. 'Sorry, I'm just really hungry.'

'Nervous energy. That pony of yours settled in at the Whites'?'

'Yep, I've decided to call her Pip.'

'Nice name.'

'The Whites have invited me to go around

tomorrow. I'm going to learn how to groom Pip and maybe have a ride. Is that OK?'

'That should be fine for an hour or two, but we do have some errands to run: school starts next Monday, and you'll need a uniform and books.'

Jade frowned; she didn't want to think about that.

'It's not the end of the world, Jade. You know that Mr White used to teach at Flaxton School?'

'No. What did he teach?'

'English, I think. Or history? Anyway, he's all right, isn't he? And there are bound to be other teachers you'll get on with. Not to mention kids — it'll be your chance to make some new friends.'

'Making friends isn't that easy,' Jade said, thinking about Rose back in Auckland. She wondered what Rose would think of Pip; while they'd both read pony books, Rose was definitely a city girl.

'I know, love, but you'll be fine. Busy, what with Pip and getting used to the new school — but busy is good.' Granddad paused. 'You got a letter from your dad this morning. I left it by your bed.'

Jade sighed. 'I'll write back tomorrow.'

# Too much to learn

*Thursday, 29 January*

*Dear Dad,*
*Thanks for writing to me. I'm glad you're OK.*
*I'm fine too. Granddad is being really kind and*
*I've already met some nice people in Flaxton.*
*School starts next Monday, so I'm going to be*
*really busy soon. I'll work hard to catch up on*
*what I missed at the end of last year and I'll try*
*to make new friends.*

*The reason why I'll be extra busy is that I've*
*now got a pony called Pip. It's sort of a long*

story, but I rescued her from the pound and she's staying in Mr White's paddock. Mr White is a nice man who got his horse-float fixed at Granddad's. When he saw that I had a pony and nowhere to keep her, he offered to graze her at his place and teach me how to look after her. Mrs White is nice, too. She's letting me use her daughter's old riding clothes. They actually have everything you need to start learning to ride — it's almost too good to be true. I know that riding costs a lot of money, but the Whites are very generous.

I'm not going to be a charity case, though. Once I've got my schoolwork under control and learnt a bit more about riding, I'm going to get a part-time job. I don't know where yet, but I am determined to look after Pip myself. I think having a pony will be really good for me. I'll learn about responsibility and stuff. Plus, I think Mr White will be a great teacher. He used to teach at Flaxton School, so he'll be good at explaining.

I'll write to you every week. One year isn't that long — we can have next Christmas together.

*Please write back!*
*Lots of love,*
*Jade*
*PS: I miss Mum and Grandma too.*

It took Jade hours to write this letter. She didn't know what to say. She was still sitting up in bed, with her bedside lamp on, finishing the letter, when her granddad came in.

'It's nearly two, Jade! Get some sleep, girl.'

'Sorry, Granddad. I'll turn my light out now,' she said, quickly putting the letter away.

'Make sure you do. We've got lots to do tomorrow.'

Jade was woken at seven by the sun glowing orange through the brown curtains. She was still tired, but excited about her riding lesson.

Jade wasn't vain, but that morning she dressed carefully, putting on her newest dark blue jeans and a clean, green T-shirt with a white four-leaf clover on the front. She even found matching socks and tried to rub the dust and grass stains off her red Converse sneakers. Going to the bathroom to sluice the sleep out of her eyes, Jade looked in the little mirror above the sink. She didn't look horsey yet, she thought, and her hair was a mess. Back in her room, she found a hair tie and pulled her wavy dark-brown hair back into a tight plait. That was better. Now she felt tidier.

As usual, her granddad was up before her and making toast and tea.

'You ready to go and sort out your school uniform?' he asked, passing her a steaming mug of milky tea.

'Yeah, I suppose so,' Jade said. 'But the shops won't be open yet, will they?'

'We're not going to the shops. Do you remember your grandma's friend Joan? She's offered us her granddaughter's old uniform. Still good as new apparently. Joan's an early riser, so when you've finished your breakfast I reckon we'll head round. That'll give you more time with Pip, won't it?' Granddad smiled at Jade.

'Yeah, it will. Thanks, Granddad.'

It was a fifteen-minute drive to Joan's. Her cottage was one block away from Flaxton's main road and doubled as a second-hand book shop and haberdashery. Granddad was right: Joan was an early riser — at just eight in the morning, the sign in her shop door already said *OPEN*.

Inside, the shop smelled mustily of roses. There were dusty dolls in the window display, baskets of skeins of wool in the corners, and shelves of books lining the walls. Behind the counter sat a woman about Granddad's age, with hennaed hair and wearing a fluffy mauve cardigan.

'Ed!' she said, looking up from her book and putting down her coffee mug. 'And you must be Jade — lovely to meet you.' She held out a hand with long scarlet fingernails, and Jade shook it shyly. 'Come out the back and I'll show you the uniform. Tracey was about your size, perhaps slightly shorter. Coffee, Ed?'

'No thanks, Joan. Just finished a cuppa at home.'

'Are you sure? The kettle's just boiled.'

As Granddad drank a cup of coffee that he didn't really want, Jade tried on a plaid, mustard-coloured summer tunic, a scratchy navy-blue jersey, and a blue-and-yellow tartan kilt with a fawn blouse for winter. As if that wasn't enough, Joan also threw some blue woollen tights and a very faded PE uniform over the curtain for Jade to try on.

'I made this little changing room for my clients; I also make ball dresses, you see. When you're a bit older, you can come back for something a bit more glam than a kilt. Isn't that right, Ed?'

'We'll see.'

'Oh, that's right — you might be back up in Auckland after this year, mightn't you?' Joan asked Jade as she emerged from the changing room, back in her own clothes. Joan's face was grimacing sadly, 'What a lot you've had to go through for one so young!'

Jade didn't know what to say to this, so she just gave a slight nod.

'Oh dear, I hope I haven't upset you, darling. You look like a strong wee thing and you've got a wonderful grandfather. Flaxton's not such a bad place, either.'

Jade objected to being called a 'wee thing', so decided not to dignify Joan's speech with an answer.

'Say thanks for the uniform, Jade,' Granddad said quietly, as he tried to make his way to the front of the shop.

'Thanks,' Jade said, even more quietly.

'A pleasure. Do come back if you need anything, dear. If you need a woman to talk to, I'm here.' Joan's beaming face seemed entirely unaware of Jade's hostility.

'She means well,' Granddad said, as they drove to Mr White's. 'I know she could've been more sensitive, but you've got to realize that she's a friend. And I couldn't have afforded all of this new,' he added, motioning to the bag of hand-me-down uniform at Jade's feet.

'I know, Granddad. I did try to be grateful, but if I'd opened my mouth I might've said something rude.'

Granddad chuckled. 'Just remember who your

friends are and try to be polite. People will cut you some slack because we have been through a lot, but do try to be friendly. It's the only way you'll fit in.'

After this uncharacteristically long lecture, Granddad was quiet until he dropped Jade off at the Whites' gate.

'Give me a call when you need a ride home — we can't have Mr White ferrying you back and forth all the time.'

'Thanks. I will.'

Around at the yards, Jade found Brandy and Hamlet already tied to the fence. Up close they were huge. When Jade put out her hand to stroke Hamlet's nose, it nearly disappeared into his mouth.

'Keep your hand flat!' Mr White called, as he came through the back gate from his house. 'Ham's greedy — he'll nip if he gets the chance, but if you hold your hand flat he'll just lick.'

Mr White was right and Jade laughed as Hamlet

slobbered over her hand and up her arm.

'Right,' Mr White said, approaching with a proper lead rope. 'Shall we start with catching your pony, then?' Jade nodded vigorously. 'Jolly good. Perhaps just watch me this first time.'

Jade watched as Mr White, with a carrot held out in one hand and the lead rope held behind his back in the other, walked towards Pip, who was in the far corner of the paddock, watching suspiciously.

'Hello, girl,' Mr White said softly as he got closer.

To Jade's relief, Pip stopped grazing and started trotting towards Mr White.

'She wants to be caught!' Jade said, pleased.

'Don't speak too soon,' Mr White said as Pip trotted up to him and then cantered straight past and around him in a circle. 'She's playing with us.' He stopped and stood still, waiting for the pony to settle down. Having completed a full circle around Mr White, Pip finally came over and nuzzled at the carrot. Mr White clipped the lead rope onto the halter and led the pony down to the yards, to tie her up next to the horses.

'Just one night filling her belly with rich grass and she's full of beans,' Mr White said, patting the mare's neck. 'It's good to see her with a spring in her step. Do you remember how I tied the lead rope in the float?'

'Not really, sorry. You did it so fast.'

'OK, watch me this time.' Mr White proceeded to fold the rope back and forth through the twine looped to the fence and then pull it tight. 'It's called a quick-release knot. I do it this way so that in an emergency you can untie the horse quickly, with just a pull on this loose end here — like so.' He pulled and the knot fell undone. 'Hamlet over there knows how to untie this knot, don't you, boy?' Mr White said. Jade looked over and, sure enough, Hamlet had pulled his rope free and was wandering around the yard with it dragging in the dust. 'You have a go now.'

Jade copied Mr White exactly, and it worked.

'Well done. Perfect,' he said. 'Now let's get started on the grooming. This may take some time,' he said, trying to run his fingers through Pip's tangled mane.

First, Jade learnt how to run the body brush over Pip, following the direction in which her coat grew. Pip enjoyed being brushed firmly and leaned into Jade's hand. Great clouds of dust were coming from Pip's back and rump, until both Jade and the body brush were grey with filth.

'Now you're just rubbing the dust back into her,' Mr White said. 'Try using this curry comb here to clean out the brush as you go. If there are any tough clumps of mud, like on Pip's hock, you could use the curry comb to dislodge them too, if you like.'

It took a long time and Jade's arms were aching by the end of it, but Pip eventually scrubbed up nicely. Mr White had taught Jade how to move around a horse while grooming, how to lift up the hooves and remove the caked dirt with a hoof-pick, and how to comb the mane.

'She's not like a person,' Mr White said un-necessarily, as he encouraged Jade to pull out handfuls of mane while combing. 'Notice that she's actually enjoying it? It doesn't hurt her like it would you or me.'

Finally, Jade oiled Pip's brittle hooves, trimmed the hairs at the back of her fetlocks, which Mr White said were called feathers, and even cut her tail which, until then, had been dragging along the ground.

Pip's black coat was finally shining and her four stockings were almost white.

'I'm afraid you won't be able to ride her today, Jade,' Mr White apologized. 'You may have noticed while you were picking them out, Pip's hooves are not in good condition at all. The farrier's coming around to do Ham's and Brandy's shoes this afternoon; I think we should get him to trim Pip's hooves, too. While you're just learning, she won't need shoes. But eventually . . .'

Jade felt uncomfortable. 'Farriers cost a lot, don't they?'

'It depends what they're doing. Brian Finch probably won't charge very much to trim Pip's hooves today, as he's coming anyway. But, yes, getting horses shod can cost a lot.'

'I've decided to get a part-time job once I'm settled at school,' Jade said firmly, but not managing to meet Mr White's eye.

'You just concentrate on learning about Pip and, as you say, settling in at school. You start on Monday, don't you?'

'Yeah.' Only two more days of freedom. Jade hated being reminded of this.

'You'll be fine.'

The rest of the lesson was filled with learning about tack. By one-thirty, Jade could throw the saddle and saddle blanket onto patient Pip's back in one graceful motion, then reach under her pony's belly and fasten the girth. She could also ease the snaffle into Pip's mouth and gently pull the head piece over her ears, remembering to arrange her forelock over the brow band.

'So, how do you tell if the throat lash is too tight?' Mr White tested, as he helped Jade untack her pony.

'If you can't fit four fingers held sideways,' Jade said, as if she'd been learning about bridles for years.

'Very good. You're a quick learner, Jade. And I'm also very impressed at Pip's behaviour today. Usually ponies will play up for new owners, nipping and stamping, but Pip's been an angel. I think she deserves a feed. In fact,' he said, running his palm over Pip's ribbed side, 'she needs one.'

Before going in for lunch with Mr and Mrs White, the last thing Jade learnt for the day was how to prepare Pip's feed. She took a double handful of chaff, mixed it together with a big handful of a sweet, slightly sticky mixture that smelt like cereal, which Mr White called cool feed, and added a bit of water, to stop the dust in the chaff from getting up Pip's nose.

While Pip gobbled her bucket of feed, Jade shyly sat at the Whites' table and had a ham, cheese, lettuce and tomato sandwich, with a glass of juice, an apple, and a big slice of chocolate cake to finish.

After lunch, Mrs White insisted that Jade try on some riding clothes. Abby White's hand-me-downs fitted even better than the second-hand school uniform, and, looking in the floor-to-ceiling mirror in the Whites' spare bedroom, Jade felt a lot horsier. The pale fawn jodhpurs and shiny brown leather ankle boots suited her. Even the black helmet fitted well.

'I can't thank you enough for these, Mrs White. They're perfect,' Jade said, almost overcome.

'You look wonderful. It's a pleasure to see them being used again. And, you know, just between you and me,' Mrs White whispered, 'I haven't seen Jim look this satisfied since he retired. You're doing us a favour, too, Jade.'

At dinner, Jade told her granddad in great detail about her day at the Whites'. Predictably, he wasn't all that happy about her accepting the riding clothes and letting Mr White pay for the farrier.

'But, remember what Mrs White said: I'm doing them a favour, too.' Even Jade wasn't really convinced by this, but she couldn't bear the thought of not going back the next morning and learning to ride Pip properly.

'Of course you can go back tomorrow, Jade. As long as the Whites are happy to have you, I don't mind. It's just that a pony's a big responsibility — I don't quite know what we've got ourselves into.'

That night, Jade took a long time getting to sleep as she wondered about money-making schemes. A 40-hour famine? A raffle? Giving pony rides? Working at Joan's shop? She knew these ideas were terrible, but hatching ridiculous plans was better than worrying about school or her dad.

When she finally slept, she dreamt about galloping Pip across a big open field, up and down hills. But she didn't have a saddle and kept feeling like she was going to fall off. Eventually she did end up slipping. As she fell, she woke up with a start.

'She's missed you,' Mr White said, as he and Jade watched Pip trot over to the yard to greet them. 'That's good to see — it means that she probably won't mind you having a ride today. And her hooves are much better now, too. Aren't they, girl?'

Jade groomed, saddled and bridled Pip all by herself, while Mr White got a long white rope and a whip out of the shed.

'What's that for?' Jade asked, putting her helmet on and, once again, admiring her jodhpur boots.

'This is a lunging rope and this is a lunging whip,' Mr White said, mysteriously.

'What's lunging?'

'Lunging is an excellent way to exercise a horse if, for some reason, it can't be ridden. It's also a good way of easing a horse back into riding. We don't know when Pip was last ridden, so we'll try her on the lunge first. I don't want you breaking your neck before we've even started.'

Jade watched as Mr White buckled the lunging halter and rope over Pip's bridle. Pip flicked her head up irritably but allowed Mr White to lead her into the paddock and walk her in a circle around him. He would use the long end of the whip to tickle at Pip's heels to get her to speed up, and tug gently at the rope to get her to slow down. After a bit of cajoling, he managed to get Pip going from a shambling walk to an elegant trot, though soon she broke into a canter and became over-excited. However, after turning her around and doing the same thing methodically in the other direction, Pip calmed down.

'Now, she's moving really nicely. See how her back hooves are reaching the spot where her front hooves used to be — that's called tracking up. In another life, Pip was probably a very well-schooled pony.'

Bringing Pip back to the yard and removing the lunging halter, Mr White finally asked the question Jade had been waiting for: 'Right, are you ready to mount up?'

'Yes,' Jade squeaked.

'OK, just do as I say and you'll be fine. I think Pip's been looking forward to this, too.'

Mr White showed Jade how to lift each of Pip's forelegs to stretch the skin smooth under the girth. He helped her adjust the stirrup leathers — 'make sure they're the length of your arm' — and showed her how to use an up-turned bucket as a mounting block. As carefully as she could, Jade gathered the reins and a handful of mane in her left hand, put her left foot in the stirrup-iron, held the cantle of the saddle with her right hand and threw her left leg over.

Before she knew it, Jade had both her feet in the stirrups and was sitting as straight as she could in the saddle. Pip hadn't even turned a hair.

Over the next two days, Jade learnt how to hold the reins correctly and sit in the saddle securely with her heels down and her knees in. Mr White and Pip were patient and encouraging teachers, which meant that Jade's confidence grew quickly.

'I reckon I've learnt more in the last two days than I will during this whole year of school,' Jade said, in the midst of a ravenous mouthful of sausage and mustard.

'Don't be sulky about it, Jade, and what would your mother say if she saw you talking through a mouthful of food?'

Granddad's mention of her mum took Jade by

surprise — or, rather, she was surprised that she didn't mind Granddad mentioning Mum.

'She'd tell me off,' Jade said slowly. 'She'd say, "Manners, miss!"' Jade and her granddad both smiled.

'Your school uniform ready for tomorrow, then?'

'Yep. All laid out by my bed.'

'Good girl. You'll be fine, Jade. I know you will.'

# Humiliations galore

In Joan's granddaughter Tracey's old Flaxton School tunic and a pair of brown roman sandals, Jade walked gingerly towards a building with a sign that said *Administration* on its side.

A woman with a perm and an impatient voice told her to go to the assembly hall ('Turn left as you leave, then walk straight ahead until you get to the quadrangle, then turn left and walk for about 20 metres, then turn right. You can't miss it.') and, after the introductory message from the principal, to go to Room 13 in Block G.

'That's Mrs Crawford's room; she teaches the Year 7s.'

'Thank you,' Jade said in a small voice, trying to remember the directions and stop her heart from beating so fast.

In the assembly hall, which wasn't really hard to find at all, Jade saw the mean girls who'd roller-bladed past her and Pip at the pound. They were shrieking with laughter again. As she walked past, one of them stuck out her foot. Jade was watching, though, and didn't trip. She paused and gave the girl a withering look.

'What are you looking at?' the girl said.

Jade just rolled her eyes and kept walking. *I don't know anyone here*, she thought despondently. *All I know is that I don't want to sit anywhere near those girls*. As she walked to the back of the hall and found an empty bench, she felt unfriendly eyes following her. She tried smiling at a group of girls who looked less intimidating. They smiled back briefly, then turned away and started whispering.

Mrs Crawford's room wasn't much better. There were about twenty-five boys and girls of Jade's age, who all seemed to know each other well, yelling across the room. Jade sat at the desk next to the door and pretended to look for something in her school bag. A shadow soon fell over her. Looking up, Jade saw an enormous girl, bulging out of her uniform.

'You're not from Flaxton, are you?' she said slowly.

'No,' Jade answered, not sure if this was a genuine question or an insult.

'My name's Luana.' The rest of the class had gone quiet and appeared to be watching now.

'Hi, I'm—' Jade began, but was cut off.

'I'm in charge here. You don't mess with me, OK? You know what happens if somebody messes with me?'

Jade shook her head.

'Beats! You gonna mess with me?'

'No,' Jade said softly, embarrassed that the whole room was staring at her.

Luana stopped and stared at Jade for what felt like half an hour, then waddled away.

A couple of boys started laughing, until Luana silenced them with a terrifyingly blank look.

When Mrs Crawford arrived and announced that there would be a seating plan, everyone except Jade groaned.

'Right, people, starting in the far corner next to my desk, I'd like Luana, Richard, Lucy, Rhys, Whare, Rocko, Maria, Ryan, Jade (welcome to Flaxton, Jade), Pohatu, Drina—', the list went on, but Jade stopped listening after her name was called. While her classmates whined about having to sit next to a member of the opposite sex and being separated from their friends, Jade went to her desk and almost began to relax. When she saw that the boy on her right was surreptitiously reading a *Horse Trader*, she felt even better.

'What are you reading?' she asked.

The boy jumped and quickly bundled the paper into his bag. 'None of your business.'

'I like horses, too. I've got a pony.'

'Good for you,' he said defensively. Jade decided that he probably didn't want to be seen talking to the new girl about ponies, so she understood.

Pohatu, on her left, was scribbling quietly on his pencil tin.

The morning was boring but painless, as Mrs Crawford established class rules and handed out a stationery list. But at the beginning of lunch-time, as Jade had feared, the day went downhill.

In the quad, everyone was sitting in groups talking or throwing balls around. With nothing better to do, Jade sat under a tree, ate her sandwich and tried to draw a horse on the front of her new exercise book. She was good at drawing, but getting the legs right was tricky, so she decided to draw her horse standing in long grass.

A shadow fell across her drawing, and Jade thought, *Oh, no — not Luana again!* But it wasn't; instead, two of the friendlier-looking girls from assembly stood in front of her.

'I'm Laura and this is Becca,' said the shorter one with a blonde ponytail and braces. 'You're new in Mrs Crawford's class, aren't you?'

'Um, yeah. I'm Jade.'

'Would you like to come and have lunch with us?'

'Yeah, OK,' Jade said, hoping she didn't sound

too relieved and desperate.

Laura and Becca, and their friends Sophie and Drina (who was in Jade's class), sat in the middle of the quad, sunning their legs.

'Oh look, Becca — she likes horses!' said Laura, pointing at Jade's drawing. 'Becca loves horses. In fact, she might be getting a pony for her birthday in April, isn't that right?'

Becca, a quiet girl with bright red hair and very pale skin, nodded slightly and smiled. 'Becca's shy, so I do most of the talking, don't I?' Laura laughed.

'It's a good drawing,' Becca said when Laura had stopped talking. 'Do you ride?'

'Yeah, actually I just got a pony a week ago. I'm a complete beginner, but I love horses.'

'Wow, that's so cool. My cousin has a gelding called Shady, which I've ridden a bit. Because I'm getting better and would like to do the shows next summer, Mum might get me one of my own. My cousin's in your class — Ryan.'

'I'm sitting next to him! He was reading a *Horse Trader*.'

'Yeah, that'd be him. He's been riding for ages and is really good.'

'That's awesome.'

'Don't talk about it in class, though. The other boys make fun of him — horses are girly.'

By the end of the lunch hour, Jade had found out all about Laura and Becca — Drina and Sophie were less friendly — without having to tell them too much about herself. Laura's mum and dad owned the café on the main street; she had one younger sister, Lucy, who was still at primary school, and two fox terriers called Bubble and Squeak; and Laura's dream in life was to become a small-animal vet. Becca's mum and dad had a dairy farm just out of town, and she had an older brother, Matthew, who was studying to become a vet at Massey University in Palmerston North.

All Jade had to tell them was that she'd grown up in Auckland, and that since her mother had passed away she'd been staying with her grandfather. She could tell that Laura wanted to know more, but was too polite to ask.

'Would you like to visit Pip after school?' Jade asked her new friends as the bell rang.

'I'd love to!' Becca said, grinning. 'Meet you by the bike racks at three-fifteen.'

Jade had packed her riding gear in her school bag so she wouldn't have to go back to her granddad's before heading over to Mr White's. When the last bell rang, she raced to the toilets, pulled off her uniform and slipped on her jodhpurs and a T-shirt.

'Look at you, all got-up,' Laura said, when Jade met them by the bikes.

'It was just easier getting changed here — I don't keep Pip at home, because there's no room,' Jade said, embarrassed.

'No, you look cool. That's all I meant,' Laura said, patting Jade's shoulder.

They'd nearly finished the long walk to Mr White's when the familiar whirr of roller-blades on tarmac approached from behind. *Oh, no!* Jade thought.

'Look, it's the horse-lover!' the girl with bleached hair crowed. 'We know all about you, horse girl.'

Jade went cold but kept walking.

'Go away, Natasha,' Laura said, staying close to Jade.

'You don't know who your new friend is, Laura,' Natasha said, more quietly.

'Yes, I do. She's Jade Lennox from Auckland, who lives with her granddad on Grove Road and is way nicer than any of you tarts.' Jade was impressed at Laura's speech, but scared of what was coming.

'You don't know the half of it then, do you?' Natasha laughed. 'Where are her parents and her grandma?'

Jade felt hot, then cold. She bit the inside of her mouth. 'Shut up,' she whispered.

'What was that? Do you have something to say?'

'I said "Shut up!" '

'Why? Don't you want Laura and Becca to know that your dad's in prison for killing your mum and granny?'

Jade wanted to kick Natasha in the shin, but instead she stood stock-still and stared at the girl with the earrings and bleached hair. She was so glad she wasn't crying, that her dry eyes could stare this troublemaker down.

'I don't care who knows,' Jade said, her voice quivering just a little. 'But I'm not going to talk about it.'

'I bet you're not. Your family is a disgrace!' Jade was still staring Natasha in eye, and the bully was starting to weaken. What Becca and Laura were doing, Jade didn't know. They'd probably disappeared.

'Maybe, but I wouldn't swap places with you!' Jade said, still staring.

'Watch your back, and your little pony's too!' Natasha yelled as she bladed away.

When Jade turned around, she saw that her new friends were still there, standing on the grass verge, waiting for her.

Jade was exhilarated after the argument. She hadn't cried! That was a success.

'I'm sorry about that,' Jade said.

'You shouldn't be sorry!' Laura said, too quickly. 'Those girls like being mean — they thrive on it. Like parasites or something.'

'Is it true, what they said?' Becca asked, quietly, once they'd started walking again.

'Sort of,' Jade said, unable to look at her friends while she admitted it. 'Dad was speeding. Mum and Grandma were in the car when it crashed. They died.'

'Oh my gosh, I'm so sorry!' Laura said, tears welling up in her blue eyes.

'That's terrible,' Becca said, putting an arm around Jade.

'Please don't be too nice to me; I don't want to start crying. I haven't really talked about this to anyone except a counsellor in Auckland and my friend Rose.'

'When will your dad get out of prison?' Laura asked.

'Probably just before next Christmas.'

'Are you angry at him?'

'No. Well, yeah, but not really. I don't know. He's sad, too. And it was an accident.'

When they got to the paddock, Jade was relieved to see Pip waiting for her at the gate; it was as if she knew her owner would need comforting.

'Oh, she's gorgeous!' Becca cried, scratching a bit of mud off the pony's brow and patting her neck. 'Are you going to have a ride?'

'I hope so, if Mr White's around. He's teaching me how to do everything. Though I guess we could get her groomed and saddled without him.'

Becca and Laura went to the shed and fetched the tack and grooming tools while Jade put on Pip's halter and brought her into the yard. With some hints from Becca, Jade remembered how to put on the saddle and bridle. When Mr White came out and saw Pip all ready, shining from perfect grooming and tacked up correctly, he was delighted.

'Well done! You hardly need me at all now.'

'Becca, Laura, this is Mr White. He helped me save Pip from the pound and has been very generously grazing her for me. I'm pretty useless with horses, even though I love them, so he's been doing everything.'

'That's not true — look, you saddled up today just fine without me. Why don't you mount now and show me what you remember.'

Pip was in a good mood and behaved beautifully, letting Jade relax and focus on keeping her hands still and down, knees in, heels down, back straight and head up. As they rounded the corner next to the jumps, Pip broke into a trot.

'Oh!' Jade gasped, bumping in the saddle.

'Don't worry, just shorten your reins a bit — that's right — and rise and fall with the stride. Hands still! Let your elbows bend and straighten as you rise. That's not too bad at all. Now sit back, squeeze with your legs and on the inside rein, and bring her back to a walk. That's the way.'

By the end of the lesson, Jade was walking and trotting quite comfortably on both reins.

'Pip's being so good!' Jade said. 'Would you like a ride, Becca?'

'Pip's not too tired?'

'Certainly not — she could do with twice as

much exercise,' Mr White said. 'Do you ride, Becca? I thought you looked familiar. Were you at Flaxton Pony Club's Christmas gymkhana?'

'Yeah, but it was my cousin's pony.' Becca blushed slightly.

'You were at a gymkhana?' Jade was impressed.

It soon became clear that Becca was a better rider than she'd let on — even in her PE shorts, she was sitting in the saddle nicely. Although Jade was a bit envious, she couldn't help but enjoy watching Pip moving so well.

'Why don't you try her over that little criss-cross, Becca?' Mr White said. 'I have a suspicion that she might have done a bit of jumping in the past.'

'OK.' Becca cantered Pip slowly in a circle and pointed her at the criss-cross. As horse and rider popped neatly over it, Laura and Jade clapped. The jump had excited Pip, though, who'd sped up and thrown her head in the air.

'Just sit back and pull her in a circle, Becca,' Mr White said calmly. 'I think she enjoyed that.'

When Becca had quietened Pip down and

brought her back to the yard, her pale cheeks were flushed. 'Thanks, Jade, that was great.'

'You're welcome. You're much, much better than me.'

'What? You've only been riding for a week, haven't you? I've been doing it on and off for the last year. You're doing really well for a beginner.' This could have come out patronizingly, but from Becca it only made Jade feel good.

At dinner that night, Jade chatted non-stop to her bemused grandfather about school, Pip, her new friends and even about the nasty Natasha.

'How did she know about our business?' he said sharply, when Jade had finished her story.

'I don't know. Someone must've gossiped. But I think it's OK now. I told her what I thought of her.'

Granddad smiled. 'Good for you, girl. And I'm happy that you've made friends.'

That night was the first properly peaceful sleep that Granddad and Jade had had since her arrival.

# The fall

*Sunday, 15 March*

*Dear Dad,*
*I should be writing a book report for Mrs Crawford, but I'd rather write you a letter instead. Actually, I've almost finished the book report and I've done all my maths homework, so I deserve a break. After I've finished this letter I'm going to Mr White's to exercise Pip. Mr White says we're both coming along in leaps and bounds.*

*Mr White is a nice man, Dad. I know I should*

be paying for things like grazing and hoof oil, but he won't let me. He and Mrs White keep saying that they like having me and Pip around. Granddad doesn't like it much, I don't think. I promise I'll get a job in the next holidays. I really want to start paying Pip's way.

Pip's so cool. I haven't fallen off yet, which Becca and Mr White said is amazing. You usually fall off at least once in the first month, apparently. Becca is a really good rider and her mum is getting her a pony for her birthday in April. We're all really excited.

Sorry that this letter is mostly about ponies. I'll send you a photo of me and Pip in the next letter.

I hope you're still OK. Did you get the magazines and stuff that me and Granddad sent?

Please write back soon.

Lots of love,

Jade

This letter was written and posted quickly, as Jade was keen to get back to the paddock and continue where she and Pip had left off yesterday.

When she arrived at the Whites', Mrs White was out in the yard, stroking Hamlet's cheek.

'Oh, Jade, I'm glad to see you!' she said, her face drawn.

'What's happened?' Jade asked, noticing now that Pip and Brandy weren't in the paddock. 'Where are the others?'

'They got out in the night — someone left the gate open.'

'It wasn't me! I'm very careful about that.'

'I know, dear, I wasn't blaming you,' Mrs White said. 'We're careful to check the gate too. Someone must have opened it during the night. Jim's beside himself — he's out looking for the horses now.'

Jade started to feel ill. 'It *is* my fault,' she said quietly. 'I argued with some girls from school. They know I keep Pip here — they even said that I should watch her back!'

Mrs White climbed over the fence, out of the distressed Hamlet's yard, and gave Jade a firm hug.

'It's *not* your fault — even if it were those girls, which I can well believe. Some children at Flaxton

School are as rough as guts.' Mrs White paused. Jade had never heard her sound anything but sweet before now. 'Anyway, we've done all we can for now. I've called our friends with horses, and Olivia at the pound, asking them to keep their eyes open. And Jim's out with the horse-float. Why don't you wait here and keep Hamlet company? He must have been asleep while the others cantered out the gate — or maybe you just didn't want to miss breakfast, eh, Hammy?'

Jade sat on the fence, stroking Hamlet's neck and feeding him more hay than he needed all after-noon. Twice Mrs White offered her lunch, but Jade couldn't eat.

As afternoon turned to evening, and Mr White still hadn't turned up, Mrs White suggested that Jade go home.

'No,' Jade said, 'I'd rather wait.' As she said this, Mr White's ute pulled into the driveway. He parked next to Mrs White and Jade. Hamlet whinnied at the float, but there was no answer.

'You didn't find them?' Jade asked.

'I'm sorry, Jade. I tried.'

Seeing Mr White's weary face nearly set off the tears Jade had been holding back all day. Feeling guilty and defeated, she called her granddad for a ride home.

That night, as Jade sat grimly at the dinner table, pushing a chicken drumstick around her plate, the phone rang. She leapt up, knocking her chair over, and ran to answer it.

'Hello?'

'Jade, love, is your granddad in?' It was Joan.

'Yeah, I'll just get him,' Jade muttered. 'Joan on the phone,' she called.

Jade could have sworn that her granddad winced. 'Tell her I'm just finishing my tea — I'll give her a bell in half an hour.'

Jade passed on the message and hung up. She had just sat down when the phone rang again.

'Hello,' she said despondently, expecting Joan.

'Jade, good news!' Mr White said.

'They're back?'

'Almost. We've just had a call from a woman who lives way down Amberley Road. She went out to feed her horses tonight and found our two loitering at the fence. She says they're both fine — no cuts or scrapes, which is very lucky.'

'That's amazing!' Jade said. 'How did she know your number?'

'Abby painted our phone number on Brandy's rug, thank goodness, otherwise they might have been at the pound by now. Anyway, they're safe for tonight and I'll collect them in the morning.'

'Thanks for letting me know. I'll be around first thing tomorrow.'

Jade returned to her dinner, finally able to eat.

When Jade arrived at nine the next morning, Mr White was out in the yards with Brandy and Pip, while the farrier filed Hamlet's near hind hoof.

'You must've been up early. I was hoping to help you collect them,' Jade said to Mr White, after she'd flung her arms around Pip's neck and given her a big hug.

'That's a nice wee horse you've got there,' said the farrier, watching Jade with Pip. 'As I was saying to Jim last weekend, she looks familiar.' Before Jade could reply, Mr White spoke.

'I had to get them early, because Brian here was coming around to fix Ham's foot — he cast a shoe during all the excitement.'

*She's not a horse, she's a pony*, Jade thought, wondering where Mr Finch had seen Pip before.

'Pity about the four white stockings, though,' the farrier said, hoisting up Hamlet's leg again and fitting the shoe against the hoof.

'I like her white stockings,' Jade said, slightly outraged.

'Yeah, but the hooves are a problem — white hooves are weak hooves. Do you jump her?'

'I want to,' Jade said firmly. 'And I think we're almost ready.' Mr White laughed at this.

'Well, you'll want to get some shoes on her when you start going in for the shows. I'm sure I've shod her in the past.'

'Really?' Mr White said, interested. 'There's a bit of a story about how Jade acquired Pip.' He filled Mr Finch in on the rescue from the pound.

'Well, you've certainly got some gumption,' Mr Finch chuckled. Jade didn't reply, but made up her mind to look up 'gumption' in the dictionary as soon as she got home.

With both Mr White and the farrier present, Jade wanted to show off. Last week she and Pip had trotted elegantly over poles on the ground. Trotting in a circle around the jumps now, using her legs and squeezing on her inside rein to get Pip to bend in the right direction, Jade was disappointed that her pony was sluggish. It was a warm day and the other horses were relaxing in the yards, but still, Jade thought, couldn't Pip be as enthusiastic as her rider?

Jade rode towards the criss-cross. It was the smallest, most approachable jump in the paddock. Pip didn't seem to be focusing on the task ahead of her; instead, she cantered lazily towards the obstacle, took a long stride and then a tiny one, which surprised Jade. Both horse and rider cleared the little jump, but neither was graceful.

Mr White laughed pleasantly. 'Got that one a bit wrong, didn't you? Why don't you do some more schooling with her, Jade? It's hot and I don't think Pip's in the mood for jumping today; besides, you're not quite ready yet, yourself.'

Jade was angry, but tried not to show it. 'OK,' she said, 'but I just want to jump this one properly first. I want to end on a good note.'

As they approached the jump again, Pip was still lethargic. Noticing out of the corner of her eye that the farrier had stopped working and was watching her now, Jade decided to give Pip a no-nonsense tap on the rump with the whip. She'd never done this before and clumsily hit her pony harder than she'd intended. The strike of the whip distracted Pip from the jump. She bucked angrily and ran straight through the criss-cross, scattering poles right and left.

Midway through the buck, Jade had lost her stirrups. Her reins were loose after she'd used the whip, too. As Pip careered through the jump, Jade toppled off, landing awkwardly on the jump stand.

The fall had winded her, but she got up straight away, ashamed of herself. Pip had trotted back to the yards to seek solace with Brandy and Hamlet.

'Are you OK?' Mr White asked as Jade approached.

'Yeah, just embarrassed. I deserved that: Pip didn't do anything wrong.'

'You're right there,' the farrier chipped in, irritating Jade. 'First fall, was it?'

'Yep.'

'You landed pretty well. That's an important skill to learn.' Jade smiled and forgave Mr Finch for his last comment.

'You're holding your wrist, Jade. Are you sure you're all right?' Mr White asked.

Jade looked down and saw that her left hand was indeed clutching her right wrist. She let go, and as her arm swung down she felt a hot pain. 'It is a bit sore, actually. I thought I was fine, but my arm feels hot.'

'It's not your writing hand, is it?' Mr White asked

as he drove her to the doctor. He'd untacked Pip quickly and left Mr Finch to finish off Hamlet's shoe. Again, Jade felt embarrassed.

'No. I'm left-handed.'

'Can you wiggle your fingers?'

Jade tried. 'Yes, but it hurts.'

'Probably a minor sprain, then.'

Mr White, as usual, was right. The doctor at the Flaxton clinic bandaged her wrist up tightly, put it in a sling and gave her some painkillers.

'Will I be able to ride?' Jade asked the doctor.

'I'd give it at least a week to rest. You don't want to make it worse.'

Crestfallen, Jade let Mr White drive her home.

'I've undone all the good work we did last week,' Jade said, gloomily.

'Yes.' Mr White's agreement surprised her.

'I should've listened to you when you told me to stop jumping.'

'Yes.'

Jade looked so sad that Mr White patted her shoulder gently. 'It's not the end of the world. Pip will have forgiven you in a week's time. At least, we should hope so, because I was planning to take you both to a pony club rally.'

'Pony club?' Jade's face lit up.

'Yes, they're meeting next Sunday. If you're both up for it, I thought we could enrol you. Now that you've learnt the basics I think you'd benefit from some competition and teaching. Would you like that?'

'I'd love it! But they'll all be better than me, won't they?'

'I wouldn't suggest it if I didn't think you could cope.'

The prospect of pony club cheered Jade up. She stopped scolding herself for riding Pip badly, and falling off in front of Brian Finch, and started thinking about what pony club might involve.

Once, when Jade was younger, she and her family had driven past the Flaxton Pony Club grounds. There must have been a gymkhana on, because the paddock was filled with shining ponies and young riders wearing spotless jodhpurs, gleaming boots and coloured sweatshirts. Some were riding in circles, others were racing each other, weaving between poles, and some were jumping. The paint was peeling off the jump rails, but the course still looked professional and exciting with its red-and-white flags and judges' truck.

Jade and her mum had both admired the pony club.

'It's a shame we live in the city, isn't it?' her mum had said. 'If we lived here, you could learn to ride.'

'Let's move here,' Jade had said, not taking her eyes off the riders.

'You'd miss your friends, and Dad and I wouldn't have jobs. You wouldn't get to go to the movies as often, either. Sometimes I wish you could've grown up in the countryside, but Auckland's not so bad, is it?'

*And now I'm here*, Jade thought, confused.

To take her mind off the memories, she made lunch for her and her granddad, buttering bread, slicing tomatoes, rinsing lettuce and frying bacon. It was difficult working with one arm, but it provided a good distraction. As she arranged the sandwiches on plates, her granddad came in, carrying letters.

'That bacon smells lovely. You're a good girl. But what've you done to your arm, Jade?' her granddad said, looking up from the post and seeing the sling.

'I had my first fall off Pip,' Jade said, almost proudly. 'It was all my fault, but I've only sprained my wrist. It's not so bad really.'

'Crikey, girl, and you still managed to make us some lunch? You take it easy this afternoon, you hear?'

Jade nodded.

'There's a letter here for you — from your friend Rose, by the looks.'

'Really? Cool!' Jade took the letter and tried to rip it open with her teeth.

'Let me do that for you,' her granddad said, chuckling.

It was a quiet, sombre lunch, with Jade poring

over Rose's letter and her granddad leafing through the bills.

'Bad news?' her granddad asked, seeing that Jade was frowning.

'No, good news, really. Rose has invited me to stay with her in Auckland over the holidays.'

'That'll be nice — you can see your old friends.'

'Yeah, I guess. It's just that Becca might have a pony too by then, and I don't want to leave Pip for two weeks.'

Granddad could see that Jade was more upset about this than she was letting on. He understood that returning to Auckland would be tough for her, having to spend time with kids who knew what she'd been through and might not be gentle about it.

'I'm sure Mr White would keep an eye on Pip,' he said, slowly.

'I know he would, but that's not the point!' Jade snapped. 'I need to keep riding if I'm going to be good enough for next season's shows.'

'I see. But you'd quite like to catch up with Rose?'

'Yes, I think so.'

'Well, why don't you invite her to stay here?' As he said this, Granddad was wondering how he'd cope with two eleven-year-old girls for a whole week.

'You wouldn't mind? Thank you so much, Granddad!' Jade's mood had changed entirely. She leapt up and kissed her granddad's cheek, chattering away now about what she and Rose would get up to.

'Rose really wanted to meet Pip, and now I can teach her to ride a bit, too. I bet she'll like Laura and Becca. We can all hang out at Laura's café together. It'll be wicked.'

'Wicked?' Granddad shook his head.

A week is a long time when you have your arm in a sling and wish you could ride your pony. Although Jade enjoyed watching Becca exercising Pip, she itched to get back in the saddle herself.

'What if I've forgotten how to ride? I'll look like a fool in front of Rose,' Jade complained for the umpteenth time to Laura, as they both sat on the fence, watching Becca.

'You're worrying too much,' said Laura. 'Can Rose ride?'

'No.'

'Well, she won't know if you're doing it right or not. And if she's a real friend she won't care anyway. Did you go to school with her in Auckland?'

'Yeah. Though we've known each other since we were babies — our mums were next to each other in hospital when we were born.'

'Wow, you're like twins then.' Laura sounded slightly jealous.

'It feels like that sometimes.'

Laura slipped off the fence and bent down to pat Bubble and Squeak, who'd come along for the walk. 'She might not like staying in dumb little Flaxton after Auckland.'

'It's only for a couple of weeks — and she'll have us and Pip to entertain her. Who needs the city when you've got a pony?'

Laura didn't say anything, but looked worried.

# Pony club

On Friday afternoon Jade's spirits were high. Mrs Crawford had given the class an extension on their maths homework until the following Wednesday, the wrist was only a little stiff now, and pony club was only a couple of days away.

She raced around to Mr White's in record time, not stopping for a hot chocolate at Laura's café.

Anticipating Jade's eagerness, Mr White had already caught Pip and tied her up in the yard. Hamlet was tied up next to her.

'Are you going to ride, too?' Jade asked.

'It's such a nice afternoon, so I thought, *Why*

*not?* Plus, I want to make sure that Pip doesn't mind riding near other horses. I'm sure she'll be fine, but better to be safe than sorry, especially with pony club on Sunday.'

As they'd hoped, Pip was fine riding behind Hamlet. In fact, she behaved angelically, bending nicely as she turned the corners, cantering on the right leg every time and accepting the bit.

'A week off seems to have done her good,' Jade said, surprised.

'You're forgetting that Becca has been riding her all week. That might have something to do with it, too.'

'Because she's better than me?' Jade looked hurt.

'Well, more experienced. Or perhaps Pip's just glad to have you back,' Mr White said hurriedly, seeing that he'd offended Jade. 'Look, why don't we go for a road ride, seeing as I've got Hamlet here?'

Setting off along the wide grass verge cheered

Jade up immensely. She even forgot about the nagging ache in her wrist.

As they turned left at the end of the road, Jade saw Natasha and her roller-blading posse.

'Oh no,' Jade whispered. 'Can we please ride to the pony club and have a look?' She turned around in her saddle to ask Mr White. The pony club grounds were in the opposite direction, away from the bullies.

'It's a bit far, really. And the road's too busy. You'll see it soon enough, anyway. Can you be around here at eight tomorrow morning?'

'Of course! I can't wait. It's just . . .' Jade felt pathetic saying it, 'I don't want to ride past those girls.'

'Their roller-blades might upset the horses, but if you keep your heels down and sit deep in the saddle, you'll be fine.'

'No, that's not what I mean,' Jade said, exasperated. 'They hate me and Pip — I think they were the ones who opened the gate.'

'Are you sure?' Mr White asked. He listened attentively as Jade told him the whole story.

'Right,' he said sternly, when she'd finished. 'You don't mind having a little canter, do you?' Before Jade could answer, Mr White had urged Hamlet into a creaking trot, then a canter. Jade followed, excited. As they reached the girls, the horses were racing.

'Out of our way, please!' Mr White bellowed, pointing a now-impressive Hamlet straight at the group.

The girls screamed, blading away in all directions. In her haste, Natasha fell in the ditch.

'Watch out, you mental perv!' she yelled, struggling to stand up, but not quite managing with her roller-blades in the muddy grass.

At this, Mr White pulled Hamlet to a halt and turned him around.

'Mind your manners, Natasha,' he growled. 'And if I ever find that someone has opened the gate to my paddock again, or so much as laid a finger on my horses, I will call the police *and* I will call your mother.'

For once, Natasha did not get the last word. Jade and Mr White jogged away, on their now thoroughly excited horses, without receiving any more abuse.

'I suggest that you don't ever do anything like that again,' Mr White said, when they were out of earshot of the girls. 'I'm sorry — it was extremely foolish of me, cantering off like that. Is your wrist all right?'

'It's fine,' Jade said, still stunned at what had just occurred. 'Thank you!'

'My pleasure,' Mr White said, smiling slightly.

Jade woke the following morning at seven, happier than she'd been in months. Pulling back the faded brown curtains, she was disappointed to find the day grey and drizzly. It wasn't raining heavily, though, so she pulled on her pristine jodhpurs, boots, T-shirt and jersey that she'd got ready the night before, and went to the kitchen to make herself breakfast. Walking past her granddad's room, she heard only snoring so didn't bother asking if he'd like a cup of tea.

The walk to the Whites' house was long and

grim. By the time Jade arrived, she was both flushed and bedraggled and didn't look nearly as sophisticated as she'd hoped.

The horse-float was attached to the ute and the shed door was rolled up, but there was no sign of Mr White. Jade caught Pip and tied her up in the yard, then went and knocked on the Whites' back door. Mrs White opened it and ushered Jade inside.

'Hello, Jade, would you like a Milo? Not the best weather, is it?'

'Yes, please. No, it isn't,' Jade mumbled, confused. 'Where's Mr White?'

'Well, to be honest, he's put his back out — all that gallivanting around chasing young girls yesterday,' Mrs White said, laughing shrilly. 'But he's determined to take you to pony club. I'd do it, except I don't like driving with the float on.'

'Oh,' Jade said, knowing that she should probably say that pony club wasn't that important and Mr White should really just rest.

'Would you mind awfully, Jade, if you missed pony club this morning? I don't think Jim should be going anywhere.'

'Nonsense!' Mr White said, hobbling into the kitchen. 'It's just a twinge. It'll pass soon. Anyway, you'll be the one doing the riding and grooming, won't you, Jade? I'll just have to sit in the ute.'

'Promise that you won't try and lift jump stands or anything,' Mrs White told him firmly, frowning.

'I'll hardly leave the driver's seat,' Mr White said.

'Watch him for me, Jade,' Mrs White said as they finished their hot drinks and went out to the ute.

Jade made sure that there was nothing for Mr White to do. She groomed Pip quickly and thoroughly, tacked her up correctly and mounted, somewhat inelegantly, off the side of the horse-float.

'Go and sit in the ute, I'm fine,' Jade kept telling Mr White, but he insisted on walking with her over to the group of ponies and parents assembled outside a shed. And, if she was being honest, Jade was glad that she wouldn't have to ride over alone and introduce herself to the other riders, all of whom seemed to be wearing the same pale blue sweatshirt.

As they approached, Jade recognized Ryan from her class. He was sitting on a handsome liver chestnut gelding, a bit smaller than Pip, and talking to an older girl on a beautiful bay.

'Hi,' Jade said shyly, riding up to Ryan and the girl. Fortunately, Pip had stopped neighing and pulling at the reins; now that she was closer to the other horses the only evidence of her excitement was her pricked ears.

'Hi, Jade,' Ryan said, more relaxed than in class, but still a little aloof.

The other girl gave Ryan a 'who's she?' look, and he said, 'This is Jade — we're in the same class at Flaxton. I didn't know you had a horse, Jade.'

'I'm sure I told you,' Jade said quietly. 'What's your name?' she asked the girl.

'Amanda,' the girl said, curtly.

'So you already know Ryan and Amanda? Good,' Mr White said, oblivious of how uncomfortable Jade was feeling. 'They're both very slick showjumpers — watching them will be a good way to learn.'

Amanda looked pleased. 'So you're just learning?' she asked.

'Yeah,' Jade said, clenching her teeth.

The riders were soon split into groups according to experience, and Jade was able to leave Amanda and Ryan. She was, to her embarrassment but also relief, in the baby class. Riding around in a circle with six-year-olds on Shetland ponies was, when Jade stopped being vain, quite relaxing. The instructor, a young woman called Megan, had a soft voice and was encouraging.

'Jade, you're doing very well — but I guess Jim has already taught you the basic aids. Just remember to keep your heels down and your legs back a little bit. Don't shove them forward like a cowboy. That's better.'

There was no jumping or galloping around, but they did have a bending-and-turning race as a treat at the end of the hour. Jade had never tried this before, yet somehow Pip knew what to do, weaving nimbly between the white poles, turning sharply at the end and cantering towards the finish. Partly due to Pip's prowess and partly due to her size next to the tiny ponies, Jade won the race. She did finish up on Pip's neck, grabbing a fistful of mane to steady herself, but she won.

'Pip's done this before,' the instructor said, smiling. 'Come gymkhana season, you could be quite the winning team.'

Jade beamed and was feeling happy until she and the littlies went for a warm-down walk around the paddock and passed Amanda and Ryan. As she watched the more experienced riders pointing their ponies at a terrifying jump — a large log at the top of a hill, followed by a ditch at the bottom of the hill — Jade was both intimidated and jealous.

'That's the C$^+$-certificate group,' Megan explained. 'They're doing some cross-country practice.'

'What's C$^+$ Certificate?' Jade asked.

'Well,' Megan said, 'if you're serious about pony

club, you can take exams to test your horsemanship. The first is called the D Certificate — you'll be ready for that soon. It tests your ability to control and care for your pony. Then, as you become more confident and knowledgeable, you can go for your $D^+$, C, $C^+$, B, A and H certificates.'

On the way back to the Whites', Jade was feeling tired and relaxed.

'Did you enjoy that, Jade?' Mr White asked.

'Yes, I did. And I think I'd like to get my D Certificate.'

'Excellent. I thought you might. Remind me to lend you Abby's old Pony Club manuals; they'll give you more information about that.' Mr White winced.

'Are you OK?'

'Just a twinge. I'll certainly be better in a fortnight for the next rally.' He gave Jade a pained smile.

'A fortnight? Rose will be here then!'

'Bring her along. It might be interesting for her.'

As Jade put Pip in the paddock and gave her some hay, she tried to imagine Rose enjoying pony club. For the first time, she started to realize what Laura was worrying about.

# Becca's birthday present

'Why don't you go into town after school today and have a look? If you see something Becca would like, I'll give you the money for it,' Jade's granddad said.

'I don't know what she'd like! And she'll be with me after school,' Jade shouted down the hallway from the bathroom. She was running late for school and trying to brush her hair and her teeth at the same time.

'If she's with you, you could ask her what she'd like.'

'Granddad! It should be a surprise.'

'Take your toothbrush out of your mouth while

you're talking!' Granddad was feeling out of his depth discussing how much to spend on a birthday present for an eleven-going-on-twelve-year-old who wasn't even his granddaughter. 'What happened to it being the thought that counts?' he said quietly, in a voice that made Jade feel guilty for fussing.

'You're right. I'm sure fifteen dollars will be enough — and I'll ask Laura what she's getting Becca. Anyway, whatever it is, it won't be as good as what her parents are buying her.'

'You and your ponies, I don't know,' Granddad said gruffly, pulling a twenty-dollar note out of his wallet. 'You know where the saddlery is, don't you?'

'No! You never told me there was a saddlery in town!'

'You haven't needed one yet, the Whites have been so generous. If you come here straight after school today, I'll take you. There might be something small there Becca could use.'

When Jade told Laura about the saddlery at morning break, both girls got quite excited. Laura had been planning to give Becca a *Horse and Pony* magazine and some nail polish from the chemist, but dandy brushes, hoof oil and saddle soap seemed much more appropriate.

'Are you sure she hasn't got these things already? I mean, if her parents are buying Dusty for her, they've probably bought grooming tools, too,' Jade worried.

'We'll have to do some detective work,' Laura said.

Dusty, a pretty dun pony of about 14 hands, was going to be Becca's big birthday present. Her mother had driven her to Dannevirke twice to try the pony, which used to belong to the McAlpine family, Olivia McAlpine specifically. Olivia was, according to Becca, one of the best young riders in the province.

'It was scary having to ride her pony in front of her. But Dusty was beautiful! I'm so lucky . . .' Becca, reluctant to brag, tended to trail her sentences off these days with 'I'm so lucky . . .'

The perfect pony would arrive at Becca's farm on Saturday, her birthday, which meant that Jade would have a friend at pony club on Sunday. To top it off, Rose would also be arriving, on Friday in the evening.

'I hope Rose likes horses,' Laura said to Jade as the bell rang and they wandered back to their classes, 'because I doubt we'll be talking about much else at the party.'

'I hope so, too,' Jade replied, uncertainly.

During the lunch hour, Laura, who was good at that sort of thing, managed to charm the office lady into letting her use the telephone to call Becca's mother and ask about grooming tools. Jade stayed in the quad with Becca, so as not to rouse suspicion.

'Are you riding Pip this afternoon?' Becca asked, as she unwrapped another ham and tomato sandwich. 'Because if you are, I'd love to come too.'

'Um, no, not this afternoon. I've got to run an errand for my granddad,' Jade lied terribly.

'Really?' Becca asked. 'What errand?'

'Just something boring for the garage.'

'Oh.' Becca sounded disappointed. 'You can still come to my party, though?'

'Yeah, of course! And, if you wanted to go around and ride Pip by yourself, that'd be fine. Mr White won't mind.'

'Thanks — I'm tempted, but it might be a bit weird without you there.' Becca turned to Laura as she sat down next to them. 'Where have you been?'

'Top-secret business,' Laura said, tapping the side of her nose.

'You two are so mysterious today,' Becca said, laughing.

Although Jade had been keeping up with her homework, so far this year schoolwork hadn't been one of her priorities. She'd done slightly more than the bare minimum in order to spend most of her time riding without angering her granddad, Mr White or Mrs Crawford. Balancing the load of schoolwork and horses was tiring, though, and Jade was very much looking forward to a break from book reports, maths sheets and science projects over the holidays. So that afternoon, when Mrs Crawford wrote *HOLIDAY ASSIGNMENT* on the board, Jade's blood ran cold. She wasn't alone: there were groans from all around the class. Ryan Todd, sitting next to her, looked fairly unimpressed too.

'That's enough, everyone! A holiday assignment isn't something to be dreaded, particularly not this one. I hope you'll each enjoy it, because I'm making the topic fairly flexible. You are to choose,' she said slowly, writing on the board at the same time, 'a famous person whom you admire—'

'Zac Efron!' Maria yelled.

'Yes, even Hollywood actors and musicians are allowed as subjects,' Mrs Crawford said, although with some distaste. 'But, you must be able to write a detailed biography of their life and work. There are four parts to this assignment: first, you must state why you admire your subject; second, you need to research your subject's early life, before they became famous; third, you should list their great achievements; and lastly, I'd like you to conduct an imaginary interview with your subject.'

'What if my subject's dead?' Lucy asked. 'Like Marilyn Monroe.'

'That's not a problem, Lucy. That's why I said an "imaginary" interview,' Mrs Crawford said, wearily. 'Now, everyone, during the rest of the week, please think of who you'd like to research. When you've decided, write their name next to your name on this piece of paper. The assignment is due on the first day back after the holidays.'

Laura and Granddad seemed to be in a good mood during the drive to the saddlery, which irritated Jade. They were both singing along to Johnny Cash, oblivious to her worries.

'I fell into a burning ring of fire!' They both bellowed for the third time. Jade couldn't resist. She pushed the eject button and the tape popped out, leaving only the crackle of a lack of radio reception.

'Jade! What did you do that for?' her granddad scolded.

'I'm sorry; I just can't stop worrying.'

'What are you worrying about?' Laura reached over the front seat and patted Jade's shoulder.

'Just school and Rose and stuff. I'm scared I won't have enough time for everything. I wanted the holidays to be full of riding, and it looks like I'll be stuck inside doing homework or watching videos with Rose.' Saying it out loud made it sound small and insignificant. Jade felt silly.

'What's all this schoolwork, then?' her granddad asked, parking the car outside the saddlery. 'Have you not been keeping up?'

'No, it's not that at all. Mrs Crawford's just given us this big assignment: we have to write about a famous person who we admire and I can't think of anyone.'

'What about her?' Laura said, pointing, as they all walked into the saddlery, at a poster of a pretty blonde woman wearing a jacket with a New Zealand flag sewn onto the lapel.

'That's a good idea, Laura,' Granddad said.

'Michaela lives quite nearby too. You could pay her a visit, Jade.'

'Is that Michaela Lewis?!' Jade had obviously supported the New Zealand equestrian team at the last Olympic Games and knew that Michaela Lewis had won a gold medal for showjumping, but she'd never seen the rider's face close up and without a helmet before. 'Does she really live near here?'

'Well, it's about half an hour's drive. Lovely big property. The post-and-rail fencing must have cost an arm and a leg, let alone the animals inside the fences. She's turned her riding into quite a business.'

'Oh my goodness.'

'You're star-struck!' Laura laughed. 'If you make her your assignment, your holidays will still be pretty horsey. And, if you're worried about Rose getting horsed out, she can hang out at the café with me.'

'Thanks, Laura,' Jade said, suddenly feeling unburdened, as they entered the saddlery.

Becca's mother had said that, while they had all

the grooming tools that Becca would need, extra things like horse mints, new riding gloves and horsey books would be much appreciated.

After spending much longer than Granddad had expected, Jade and Laura finally decided to pool their money and buy a beautiful red-and-white saddle blanket that had fifty per cent off. Laura, who liked doing such things, offered to take it home and wrap it.

The next day at school, before she'd even put down her bag, Jade made a beeline for the front of the class and wrote *Jade Lennox — Michaela Lewis* on the assignments list, before anyone else could steal her idea.

'You're keen, Jade,' Mrs Crawford said. 'Let's have a look at your subject.' She slid her glasses up the bridge of her nose and picked up the piece of paper. 'Excellent idea!' she said, beaming. 'Your interview might not have to be imaginary.'

Because the class was so disappointed about having to work over the holidays, Mrs Crawford gave them time each afternoon that week to begin their assignment; this meant that, for Jade, the days flew by. She googled Michaela Lewis's name and found articles dating back to her early years as a young rider, representing the province at the National Pony Club Showjumping Championships. She found photos of Arius, the beautiful flea-bitten grey Olympian, and details of how to buy other horses Michaela had trained.

When she'd gathered enough background information, Jade started drafting a list of interview questions. Although the prospect of talking to such a star was daunting, Jade couldn't stop fantasizing about visiting Michaela's farm and being shown the paddocks full of perfect horses.

On Friday afternoon, Jade spent a couple of hours with Pip before racing home to prepare for Rose's arrival. While she was sluicing the sweat mark off Pip's belly, Jade told Mr White about her assignment on Michaela Lewis.

'Do you know her very well?' Jade asked, hoping he'd say yes.

'Only in passing. We used to see her at shows with her daughter quite a bit back when Abby rode. But, no, sorry, she's not really an acquaintance. However, I've heard that she's very nice, so I imagine she'd certainly agree to an interview.'

'Do you think she'd give me a riding lesson?'

'I think that might be asking a bit much, but you never know.'

Back at home, Jade found that her granddad had already made up the camp bed in her room.

'Sorry, Granddad, I should've been home earlier and done that myself,' Jade said.

'It's no trouble. Just don't neglect Rose while she's here in favour of that pony.'

'I won't.'

'Good girl. How about we get fish and chips for tea after picking Rose up from the bus stop?'

Jade grinned. 'Sounds perfect.'

The bus was on time for once. Jade was standing

in the car park by herself because Granddad had popped down the road to the fish and chip shop. She was leaning on the Falcon just as her granddad had when she'd arrived in Flaxton. That felt like a very long time ago now.

'Jade!' Rose ran towards her, as fast as she could while dragging a suitcase on wheels behind her. She flung her arms around Jade's neck. 'I've missed you heaps!'

'I've missed you too,' Jade said, realizing it properly for the first time in weeks.

'Wow, that was a long trip. I'm famished.'

'That's good 'cause Granddad's gone to buy fish and chips,' Jade said, looking at Rose, trying to see if anything had changed since Christmas. Her hair was longer and had a pink highlight.

'How have you been *managing* in this place?' Rose asked, looking around at the empty streets and tiny, closed shops.

'Better than I thought I would when I first arrived! Pip has made it easier,' Jade said, trying not to sound too pleased.

'That's right — the pony!' Rose said. 'I can smell

fish and chips.' They both turned around and saw Granddad carrying two big, steaming parcels.

At Granddad's house, they opened the parcels on the dining table.

'I got us some ginger ale, too,' Granddad said, going over to the fridge.

'Thanks, Granddad! This is lovely.' Jade was relaxing, until she saw Rose get up and fill her glass from the cold tap.

'You don't want ginger ale?' Jade asked.

'I'm fine with water,' Rose said. 'Carbonated drinks are a bit unhealthy.'

Granddad had bought three pieces of fish, two scoops of chips, two sausages and two pineapple rings. He began dividing it out equally onto plates. 'You'll have a sausage, won't you, Rose?' he asked.

'Actually no, sorry. I'm vegetarian.'

'Since when?' Jade asked, shocked.

'Just after Christmas. It was my New Year's resolution.'

'That's OK,' Granddad said, sensing Jade's tension. 'There are plenty of chips and pineapple rings.'

Jade fell asleep before Rose, who had resorted to texting friends in Auckland when she and her old friend ran out of conversation. Rose had wanted to talk about a boy called Matt at her new school in Auckland, Jade had wanted to talk about Michaela Lewis; Rose had wanted to know if Jade missed her mum and when she'd last heard from her dad, Jade had wanted to read the Pony Club manuals she'd borrowed from the Whites.

Jade woke up less than fresh the next morning, but cool autumnal sunlight was streaming through the curtains and it was, after all, the first day of the holidays. Rose was still sleeping with the blanket over her face, so Jade tiptoed to the bathroom, had a quick shower, dressed in her jeans that were good for riding and a red cable-knit jersey, and went to the kitchen to make breakfast.

When by eight Rose still hadn't stirred, Jade decided to bring her breakfast in bed. She made a cup of tea with milk and one sugar and, remembering Rose's sudden health-consciousness, put two Weetbix, milk and a sliced banana in a bowl.

'Wakey wakey,' Jade said softly, as she put the breakfast next to the camp bed.

'What time is it?' Rose said huskily, blinking.

'Nearly quarter past eight. I've brought you some breakfast.'

'Wow, since I quit netball I haven't been up before ten on a Saturday.' Rose looked suspiciously at the bowl and ate a mouthful gingerly.

'Have you stopped eating breakfast now, too?' Jade asked.

Rose laughed guiltily. 'I have a bit, yeah. Sorry, I'm being so rude. Thanks for making me breakfast; it's very sweet of you.'

'Not really,' Jade said tersely. 'I just wanted to go and see Pip before Becca's birthday party and didn't think I should leave you behind.'

'The party's not until eleven, is it?'

'No.'

'Then we've got plenty of time. Don't stress. Just give me half an hour to shower and dress then we'll visit the prodigal pony.'

'The what?'

'Oh, never mind.'

By the time they'd walked to the Whites', Rose and Jade had stopped bickering. Rose was enjoying the fresh air and exercise, and Jade was relieved that the weather was so perfect.

'Here she is,' Jade said proudly as Pip trotted up to the gate to meet them.

'What a cutie,' Rose said, a bit shrilly. 'You're quite big, aren't you, darling?'

'Shall we have a quick ride?' Jade said to Pip, popping the pony's halter on and leading her into a yard.

'Oh, you'll get all dirty before the party,' Rose warned.

Jade laughed. 'There'll be more riding at the party — Becca's getting a new pony today.'

The ride really was brief. Jade couldn't enjoy herself when she could see Rose, in her peripheral vision, sitting on the fence picking at her nail polish, looking bored. She offered Rose a ride, but apparently the jeans Rose was wearing were too good for getting covered in horse hairs and stretched in the saddle.

'Is there going to be anyone at the party who doesn't have a pony?' Rose asked, a little nervously.

'Yeah, my friend Laura will be there. She's not that horsey; I mean, she likes horses but doesn't ride. You two should get along.'

To Jade's extreme relief, Laura adopted Rose as soon as they entered Becca's kitchen.

'You must be Rose,' she said in her friendly way. 'I love your hair!'

'Thanks,' Rose said. 'Your top's cool.' Jade looked at Laura's T-shirt and could only see stripes, but she was glad the two were getting along.

After lunch — another awkward meal for Rose because it consisted mainly of roast lamb (Becca's favourite) and then a delicious, hugely unhealthy chocolate mud-cake — the girls gathered outside to meet the famous Dusty.

'He's a bit jittery after his ride in the truck, and he hasn't got used to his new paddock yet,' Becca said as she led him out, holding the lead rope tightly.

'What a beauty!' Rose said sincerely, making Jade jealously wonder why Rose hadn't reacted that way when she saw Pip. 'He's feisty.'

'A bit *too* feisty,' Becca's mother said, smiling and helping Becca hold him. 'I'm afraid he's not in the mood to give pony rides today.'

'I don't know if I even want to ride him in front of everyone right now,' Becca said sadly.

'I reckon we should give him an hour or so to stretch his legs and settle down.'

Becca's mum was right. The girls watched *Stardust*, ate some more cake (even Rose couldn't resist a piece), and then at three o'clock went back outside to find Dusty calmly grazing.

'Now would be a good time to give you our present,' Laura said, as Becca groomed her new pony. She ran up to the house and came back a minute later with a soft, beautifully wrapped parcel.

'It's from all of us — Jade, Rose and me,' Laura said graciously, making Rose smile.

Becca opened it quickly and was delighted. 'Look, Mum! It's the most gorgeous saddle blanket.' She draped it over Dusty's back. 'It suits you, boy.'

When Becca mounted and rode in a circle, it became clear that Dusty was still rather excitable. However, she dealt with his pig roots and bucks well, sitting firmly in the saddle, never losing her cool. Eventually he started responding to her aids and rewarded her with a collected canter.

'I think that's enough for now; my arms are aching,' Becca said, patting Dusty's neck and riding back to the girls.

'You make me wish I had a pony,' Rose said wistfully, watching Becca dismount. 'He's so pretty.'

'If you're starting to feel horsey, you should come along to pony club with Jade and me tomorrow,' Becca said.

'And, if you're not feeling horsey,' Laura said, 'come to my parents' café and I'll make you a cappuccino.'

'Thanks, girls — this is so nice. I'll definitely have coffee with you next week, Laura, but pony club is an experience I just can't pass up on,' Rose said, grinning. This time, there was no sarcasm in her voice at all.

# Visiting an Olympian

The next morning, Jade didn't have to wake Rose up with breakfast in bed. She was already rifling through her backpack when Jade opened her eyes.

'Morning,' Jade said sleepily. 'Lost something?'

'Good! You're awake. I need you to help me decide what to wear to pony club.'

Jade rubbed sleep out of her eyes and wondered whether Rose was being serious. 'No one goes to pony club without jodhpurs and a tie,' she said, jokingly.

'Do you have spares?' Rose had a deep worry-line between her eyebrows.

'I'm being silly, Rosie. Just wear what you wore to Becca's yesterday.' Not wanting to continue such a trivial conversation, Jade bags-ed first shower, taking her own carefully folded pile of pony club clothes to the bathroom with her. *Really,* she thought, *it's not as if Rose is even going to be riding — why is she so worried?*

When the carefully dressed girls arrived at Mr White's, they found that he'd already brought Pip and Brandy into the yards.

'Are you going to ride at pony club today?' Jade asked, pleased.

'No, but I remembered that we'd have Rose with us and thought that an extra steed might not go astray. You'd like to have a ride, wouldn't you, Rose?'

'Definitely! Thank you so, so much!' Rose cried, stroking Brandy's nose and laughing.

'It's a shame you're wearing your good jeans,' Jade said. 'You didn't want to get horse hairs on them yesterday.'

Mrs White, who was watering the garden next to the yards, cut in: 'Rose, dear, I'm sure there's another pair of Abby's jodhs inside. Would you like to borrow those?'

'That'd be wonderful, Mrs White. Thanks!' Rose was smiling so hard it looked like her face would split. Jade groomed Pip roughly, ashamed and surprised at her jealousy.

By the time Rose had emerged from the house, looking about fifteen in not only Abby's old jodhpurs but her knee-high black boots too, Jade and Mr White had groomed both horses and put them in the float.

'How do I look?' Rose laughed, doing a quick twirl.

'Clean of horse hair,' Jade said, wiping her own dusty, sweaty brow.

If Jade had felt bad enough before pony club, once they both had mounted she felt completely inferior. On the ground, Rose had looked taller and more mature, but astride the gleaming Brandy, a good two hands higher than Pip, she looked positively regal.

'How're you doing up there?' Mr White asked, tightening Brandy's girth.

'Fine, I think,' Rose said, slightly nervously. 'I've never really ridden before, though. Only pony rides at the races when I was little. This is way cooler.'

'Yes, Brandy's certainly not a pony. She's a good sort, though — very sensible. If you do as I say, you'll be fine.'

With a complete novice to look after, Mr White had abandoned Jade entirely. She didn't feel alone for long, though, because a pretty dun pony with a familiar rider soon trotted over.

'Becca! How's Dusty? He looks gorgeous,' Jade said, gathering up her reins and walking Pip over to the meeting shed.

'He's better today. Normally horses get more excited when they go out in the truck, but the company seems to relax him. You should bring Pip over to our place and ride with me next week. Is that Rose on that horse?' Becca asked, pointing at a bay mare cantering towards them with its rider hanging around its neck.

'Oh, no!' Jade said, urging Pip to a trot. Jade managed to steer Pip in front of Brandy and grab the loose reins before Rose slid off completely. Brandy, pleased to be reunited with her paddock-mate, started to graze as if nothing had happened.

'Are you OK?' Jade asked. 'Did Brandy bolt?'

'Yeah, I'm OK. Just shaken. It was probably my fault. I wanted to come and see you and Becca.'

Mr White, who had jogged across from the horse-float, approached with a lead rope.

'Rose, are you all right?'

'Yes, Mr White. Sorry,' Rose said, sheepishly.

'That was very silly of you. Brandy isn't a tired old pony — if you kick her, she'll move and you won't be able to stop her. For the rest of the morning, you'll be on the lead rope.'

Jade tried not to look too pleased, until she caught Becca's eye and couldn't help smiling.

While Mr White led Brandy and Rose around the park, Becca and Jade spent a beautiful morning working on their paces, being quizzed on the parts of the horse and items of tack, and playing games.

The bending and turning, which Pip had won last week, ended up being Dusty's forte too. By the end of the morning, both ponies were excited and competitive. To cool down, their instructor took the group for a walk around the park, past the C$^+$-Certificate group, who were practising their galloping.

'You girls keen to get your D Certificate?' their instructor asked, walking in time with Becca and Jade.

'Yes,' Jade answered decisively for both of them.

'Good. I think you're both nearly ready. There are certificate examinations in a fortnight. If you both swot up on your theory, I think you'll pass with flying colours.'

Jade and Becca grinned at each other.

After spending a whole morning being led around, Rose had lost her initial interest in riding. She gave back the jodhpurs gladly and complained that her bottom and legs were sore from the saddle. This made it easy for Jade to suggest that

Rose spend the next few mornings with Laura, which worked out well for all of the girls. While Jade eagerly schooled Pip and practised answering questions from the *Pony Club Manual* with Mr White and Becca, Rose played with Laura's dogs, tried on silly hats in the op shop, and learnt how to froth milk using the espresso maker at the café. In the afternoons, Jade and Rose would meet back at Granddad's and lounge around together, reading, watching DVDs or baking, as they used to when they were friends in Auckland.

One afternoon, full of sugar after making a huge batch of ginger crunch, Jade felt brave. She found her granddad's phone book and looked up *Lewis, M.* There was only one, which meant that she had no choice but to call.

'I'm too scared!' Jade said. 'You do it.'

'OK,' Rose said, laughing and picking up the phone.

'No, don't! I will,' Jade grabbed the phone, making Rose roll her eyes.

'Make your mind up, scaredy-cat.'

Jade took a deep breath and dialled the number.

While it rang, she rehearsed what she'd say in her head.

'Hello, Kristen speaking,' a young voice answered.

'Hello, this is Jade Lennox. Could I please speak to Michaela Lewis?' Jade said.

'Sure, I'll just get her,' the young voice said. 'Mum!' Jade heard her shout in the background.

'Hello,' a new, deeper voice said eventually. 'Michaela speaking.'

Not sure whether to call her Michaela or Ms Lewis, Jade somehow managed to explain in a mumble that she was a young rider doing a school assignment, and she would like to conduct an interview.

'Of course — I'm flattered,' Michaela said, to Jade's surprise and relief. 'Would you like to do it over the phone now?'

'Um,' Jade said, unprepared.

'Wait; do you live locally?' Michaela asked. 'I'm free at ten-thirty on Friday morning if you'd like to come and meet Arius then?'

'That would be perfect,' Jade said.

Michaela laughed. 'OK, great. You know where to go?'

'Yep, I think I have the address here.'

'Well, see you on Friday then, Jade.'

How could it be so easy to arrange a meeting with two Olympic stars? When Granddad came in from the garage, he found the girls dancing around the living room.

'All hyped up on sugar, are we?' he said, helping himself to a piece of ginger crunch.

'Yes!' Rose squealed.

'Not just that, though,' Jade said, trying to calm down and look serious. 'I just rang an Olympian and she's invited me to visit her stables on Friday!'

'Good on you, girl,' Granddad said, giving her a little hug.

Friday was only the day after tomorrow and Jade hadn't really prepared any questions. Obviously she wanted to know how old Michaela had been when she started riding, how old Arius had been when she bought him, what training methods she used and whether she had any tips for young riders, but this was the opportunity of a lifetime — it shouldn't be wasted on mundane questions. Jade wanted to know everything.

On Thursday morning, Jade, Rose and Laura spent the day at Becca's, devising questions and admiring Dusty and Pip. Jade had gone on her first long road ride alone, all the way from Mr White's to Becca's house, while Laura's mum took Rose and Laura in her car. Pip was at first reluctant to leave Brandy and Hamlet, but soon she had her ears pricked and was enjoying trotting along the grass verges, occasionally popping over little ditches. The ride took about forty-five minutes, and by the time Jade and Pip arrived they were both ready for a big drink of water.

Jade let Pip loose in Dusty's paddock, and the two ponies cantered about together before settling down to munch on a biscuit of hay that Becca's mum had provided.

'That's a lovely big pony you've got there, Jade,' she said. 'She could almost be a horse.'

'Really?' Jade said, pleased. She'd noticed Pip

was big next to the other ponies at pony club, but hadn't given it much thought.

For lunch Becca's mum cooked the girls a big bacon and egg pie (and a smaller vegetarian one for Rose), and she made suggestions as they brainstormed interview questions.

'Would it be rude to ask how many times she's fallen off?' Becca asked.

'Probably, if you phrased it like that,' Becca's mum said. 'What if you asked whether she's had any bad falls and how she managed to get back on the horse, instead?'

Jade wrote this down. By the end of the afternoon she had filled four sides of refill paper with good suggestions.

'Are you going to ride Pip there tomorrow?' Laura asked. 'It wouldn't be much further from Mr White's than here.'

'I don't know,' Jade said. 'It might be a bit rude turning up with a sweaty pony.'

'She'd be used to it. I think you should.'

On Friday morning, while Rose was still fast asleep, Jade got up quietly, dressed in her carefully washed jodhpurs (but put an old pair of track pants over the top to keep them clean), pulled on her polished boots, filled her backpack with paper, pens and her list of questions, and walked to Mr White's. She was too excited to eat breakfast.

Pip was grazing next to Brandy when Jade got there. She looked up as if to say *It's a bit early for a ride, isn't it?* And, instead of wandering over to the yards as usual, kept grazing.

'Come on, girl,' Jade said, holding out one of the slightly shrivelled carrots from the shed. 'Please don't be naughty. It's an important day.'

Eventually Jade got Pip into the yard and gave her a good groom. Pip liked being groomed, especially around the ears, and was soon in a better mood. It was nine and the sun hadn't come out fully, so when Jade had put the finishing touches on Pip, her black coat still wasn't shining.

Jade was glad she'd cleaned Pip's tack recently — at least that looked nice. By half past nine she'd stripped off the old track pants, mounted and was riding a hesitant Pip out the Whites' gate.

There seemed to be more big milk tankers and logging trucks on the road on a Friday morning. Each time one passed, Pip shied and jogged, making Jade nervous.

'Please settle down, miss,' she said, trying to stroke the tense black neck without loosening the reins.

Jade had a good sense of direction and had listened carefully to her granddad's instructions, so, although the roads she and Pip were riding down looked unfamiliar, she didn't get lost.

After an hour of riding, Pip had calmed down. As they turned into Lane Road, where Michaela lived, Jade gasped. There were acres of beautifully kept paddocks with black-stained post-and-rail fencing. In these paddocks were eight young horses, who cantered over to the fence to greet them. The sudden company rejuvenated Pip and made her jog again, but with her neck arched and in a showy rather than a naughty manner.

Past the paddocks was a long gravel driveway down to a farmhouse and stables. Jade rode shyly past the house and around to the stables, where she found a small boy playing with a litter of Jack Russell puppies.

'Mum!' he yelled when he saw Jade. 'There's a girl on a pony!'

'Hi,' Jade said, dismounting and patting Pip's neck, thankful that she'd arrived safely. 'Those are sweet puppies.'

'It's Suzie's litter,' he said proudly, picking up a squirming puppy and cuddling it. 'This is the runt.'

'You must be Jade?' A small blonde woman wearing an old pair of boots had walked over from the house. 'This is my son, Jack. He's more into the dogs than the horses.'

'I guess he's a bit little for riding yet anyway,' Jade said, running her stirrups up the leathers, nervously.

'Oh, no,' Michaela said. 'I was riding when I was his age. And my daughter Kristen was in the saddle before she could walk. Would you like to tie your horse up?'

'Yes, please,' Jade said, conscious that she'd only

been in the saddle for four months.

Michaela led Jade around the side of the house to some yards, similar to Mr White's but carpeted with sawdust and equipped with a hay-net. Jade quickly untacked Pip, gave her a quick wipe with a twist of hay (as had been suggested to her by the *Pony Club Manual*), and then followed Michaela back into the house.

'What's your horse's name?' Michaela asked.

'Pip.'

'How long have you had her?'

'Nearly five months — not very long,' Jade said apologetically.

'She's a bit of a looker; awkward size, though.'

'What do you mean?' Jade missed the compliment completely.

'Well, just that she's a small horse or a very big pony. If you're going to compete on her, that'll complicate your entry.'

'Oh,' Jade said, disappointed and confused.

'Have you been riding long?' Michaela asked, trying to put Jade at ease.

'Only as long as I've had Pip,' Jade said sadly,

feeling out of her depth again.

'Really?' Michaela sounded genuinely surprised. 'You look so comfortable with her; most people take much longer to even learn how to move around horses, let alone how to ride them. You must have a natural aptitude.'

This time Jade didn't miss the compliment and couldn't stop smiling. While Michaela made them each a cup of tea, Jade remembered that this visit wasn't about her, and got the questions out of her bag.

'You said that you started riding when you were Jack's age — is that about four?' Jade asked.

'Three, actually; he's big for his age,' Michaela said, matter-of-factly.

'Gosh — so you always knew that you wanted to be a show-jumper?'

'No, that came later. I knew that I wanted to work with horses; my father trained racehorses and mum did a lot of hunting, so I was always encouraged to ride and was surrounded by horses. It was later on, when I was about eight, at Flaxton Pony Club, that I discovered showjumping and became a bit obsessed.'

'I go to Flaxton Pony Club!' Jade said, a little bit too loudly.

'It's a good place to learn,' Michaela said, smiling politely. 'My daughter, Kristen, used to go there, too. She's concentrating on her show-jumping, now.'

'I think I spoke to her on the phone when I called you,' Jade said, wondering how old Kristen was. 'She sounded about my age.'

'She's fourteen,' Michaela said, finishing her tea. 'How old are you?'

'Eleven.'

'Well, you've started riding quite late, but you seem to be a quick learner. Do you jump?'

'Not yet.'

'Would you like to come out and see my practice course, and meet Arius?'

'I'd love to!'

For the rest of the morning, Jade was Michaela's shadow, absorbing everything she said and trying to store every detail of the experience in her memory. She actually patted Arius's neck — he was in a back paddock, away from the road, wearing a Weatherbeeta rug.

By lunchtime, Michaela had answered all her questions, and hadn't seemed bored or offended by any of them.

'Thanks so much for your time, and for showing me Arius,' Jade said, as she saddled up Pip for the ride home.

'It was my pleasure; it's nice to see enthusiastic young riders.' Michaela checked her watch. 'Look, it's still half an hour before I have to give a lesson — if you like, I could give you some pointers for learning to jump Pip?'

Jade couldn't believe what she was hearing. 'Are you sure?'

'I wouldn't offer otherwise. Come on.'

Jade followed Michaela around to the course of enormous practice jumps and watched, relieved, as Michaela lowered two of them to criss-crosses and one to a low straight-bar, and arranged some trotting poles.

'Let's begin by getting Pip trotting nicely in a circle around the jumps,' Michaela said, in a voice that instantly relaxed both pony and rider.

Under Michaela's expert instruction, both Jade and Pip performed confidently.

'Turn left after the trot poles this time and come around to the criss-cross. Just keep trotting, that's right. When you get to the jump just lean forward slightly, and grab a handful of mane if need be.'

Jade did exactly as she was told and cleared the little jump without any trouble. Pip broke into a happy canter and flicked her head slightly.

'She liked that, but bring her back to a trot. You don't need to approach a jump fast; in fact, it's better to slow down and let your horse concentrate on their stride than to race. These are tiny for Pip anyway — she's actually got a really nice action.'

As Jade cantered slowly towards the straight-bar, she felt in complete control. Pip cleared it with 10 centimetres to spare and continued cantering elegantly around the paddock, on the right leg.

'Who's that?' Jade heard a girl say.

'We'd better call it a day now, Jade. My next

lesson's here,' Michaela said.

Jade rode up to the fence and met two girls, one on an exquisite dapple-grey gelding and the other on a roan mare with crazy eyes.

'This,' Michaela said, patting the knee of the girl on the grey, 'is Kristen. Kristen, this is Jade. She's the one who interviewed me for the school assignment.'

'Hi,' Kristen said.

'Hi,' said Jade, all of a sudden shy. 'You have a beautiful pony.'

Kristen smiled and patted her mount's neck. 'Yeah, Dorian's my darling. How long have you been riding?'

'Five months,' Jade said.

'That's not long; you looked pretty good.'

'Thanks,' Jade said, but Kristen seemed to have stopped listening.

'Mum, Piper's been a dog for Andy. You have to help her.'

Andy, the girl on the roan, looked frazzled.

'Bring her in here, Andy,' Michaela said calmly. 'Thanks, Jade! It was lovely to meet you.'

Pip needed a big feed when she got back to Mr White's, exhausted from the day's excitement. As Jade watched her big pony (or small horse) gobble her late lunch, Mr White came out of the house.

'Well, how did it go?' He could see that Jade couldn't stop smiling.

'Perfectly! You wouldn't believe it. She even gave us a jumping lesson!'

Mr White listened attentively while Jade recounted the whole story, exaggerating at times — particularly about the size of the jumps Pip had cleared.

'But,' Jade said at the end of her story, 'there was one thing Michaela said that was strange. She said Pip was an awkward size. What did she mean?'

'Yes, I'd been thinking that myself. It didn't seem worth worrying about until you started competing, but what with pony club and beginning to jump, we should probably give this problem some thought.'

'What problem?' Jade looked worried. Did Pip's size mean she was weak or sick?

'It's not a problem for small shows, but for A & P shows and other bigger events, you need to have your horse or pony registered. When you register a horse or pony, you have to give its name, colour, age and size. The problem with Pip is that she's probably 14.3 hands, which is right between pony and horse. In order to enter a pony class, your mount needs to be not larger than 14.2.'

'So I can't ride her in big shows?' Jade said, disappointed already.

'Maybe not. However, there are tricks for getting a pony down to size. You can file its hooves, or put an icepack on its withers just before it gets measured so that it shrinks down.'

'I don't want to upset Pip just so that she can compete — she's just the right size as far as I'm concerned,' Jade said decisively.

'Good, I'm glad you feel that way. But it's something to consider for next season.'

'I can still compete in pony club events and get my D Certificate?'

'Yes, of course.'

'Well, that's all I need for now.'

Jade got home late from Mr White's, feeling guilty about neglecting Rose for the whole day. She'd be going back to Auckland on Sunday and Jade had spent the whole week she was here distracted by horses.

'I'm sorry for leaving you by yourself,' Jade said, when she found Rose and her granddad cooking something spicy in the kitchen.

'Don't worry about it. I've had a great day. I slept in, then hung out with Laura, then I went shopping with your granddad. He didn't know what to cook for a vegetarian, so I said I'd make us a kidney bean chilli.'

'It smells amazing,' Jade said hungrily, realizing that the only thing she'd eaten all day was a couple of gingernuts at Michaela's house.

Over dinner, Jade retold the story of her day again — and this time with even more exaggerations.

On Sunday, Jade and her granddad saw Rose off at the bus stop. They were both a little sorry but also a little relieved as they waved goodbye to their friend. Granddad was pleased to no longer have to concern himself with vegetarian food, and Jade was glad she could focus on Pip without guilt.

The second week of the holidays flew by. In the mornings, Jade and Becca would train for their D Certificate, and in the afternoons Jade worked on her assignment. She put more effort into it than she'd ever done for a school project before. On Saturday afternoon, she printed out the finished product (nearly 2,000 words!) on Mr White's computer and showed it to him.

He flicked through, reading each page. After a few minutes he handed it back and patted her on the head. 'Splendid work,' he said sincerely.

# Certificates

The night before the D-Certificate exam, Pip and Jade stayed at Becca's house so that they could get ready together the next morning.

'I reckon we could probably sit our C Certificates, we've studied so much,' Becca said, finally putting down the *Pony Club Manual* and turning out the light at eleven.

'That'll be our next challenge,' Jade said, giggling and sliding down under the covers of the spare bed.

'Actually, there's another challenge in a few months that might come before C Certificate,' Becca said. 'The Pony Club One Day Event.'

'I wouldn't be ready for that, would I?'

'In a few months you probably would. I think we should both enter,' Becca said, with un-characteristic self-assurance.

Despite talking late into the night, the girls woke fresh and rested the next morning. After a hearty breakfast of scrambled eggs, baked tomatoes and toast, the girls groomed their ponies thoroughly, until Dusty gleamed like melting honey and Pip shone like black velvet.

When they arrived at the pony club grounds, the sun was unusually warm for autumn. Becca's mum helped them unload the ponies, then went over to talk to the other mothers while the girls saddled up.

'Should I be more nervous?' Jade asked Becca as they walked in circles, warming up before the examiner arrived.

'No,' Becca said, 'I think this'll be a breeze. And you and Pip look so good!'

'Rebecca and Jade?' said a middle-aged woman

in a tweed jacket and brown corduroy trousers.

'Yes, that's us,' Jade said.

'I'm Mrs Thompson. I'll be your examiner today. Are you ready to begin?'

The girls were confident but not over-confident. They'd prepared well. When asked to name three plants poisonous to horses, they each named five. When it came to saddling and unsaddling, they were competent to say the least. Pip and Dusty seemed to be in the mood for showing off, too, because they performed beautifully at the walk, trot and canter. Admittedly, Becca and Jade were at least four years older than the other two children sitting the exam, so it would have been embarrassing to fail. However, when the examiner handed out the certificates, Becca's throwaway comment about being ready to sit the C Certificate wasn't so unfounded.

'How long have you been riding?' Mrs Thompson asked the girls. When they replied, Mrs Thompson seemed very surprised. 'You're both quite precocious. I look forward to seeing you at the C-Certificate examination.'

When Becca's mum dropped Pip and Becca off at the Whites' and told Mr White how well the girls had done, he looked even more proud than he had the day before when Jade had shown him her assignment on Michaela Lewis.

'Well done, girls — not that I'm surprised,' he said. 'However, we mustn't get cocky. Jade, you've still got a lot of work to do before you'll be ready for the One Day Event. I assume you're keen to enter?'

'Yes, I am,' she said seriously.

'Good, I'm glad to hear it.'

The next day, the girls were back at school. If Jade hadn't had such a good assignment to hand in, she wouldn't have looked forward to it at all. Even so, the A$^+$ she was given hardly compensated for the prospect of a long term before the next holiday and the emergence of winter.

The Whites' paddocks flooded, which meant that there was nowhere good to ride, and Pip's delicate white hooves started to look suspiciously like they were getting mud fever. Mr White called the vet, and paid for his visit, which embarrassed Jade — she didn't tell her granddad about it, knowing how he'd react.

The mornings were colder, too, and the sun disappeared at five o'clock, meaning that Pip had to wear one of Brandy's hand-me-down covers, which was both too large and not quite water-proof. The early darkness also meant that after-school rides were no longer possible.

'I'm not having you walking home alone in the dark, and you can't keep asking Mr White to drive you,' her granddad scolded when Jade was late home for dinner one night.

'I wish I could drive,' Jade muttered sullenly, making her granddad laugh.

'You're going on twelve, not fifteen, miss,' he said, elbowing her in the ribs as they did the dishes. 'Which reminds me, what should I get a twelve-year-old for her birthday?'

Jade didn't want to talk about her birthday. Although a party with Laura and Becca would be nice, celebrating without her mum and dad seemed too weird. It wasn't something she felt like thinking about.

'I don't care; anything,' she said, then realized how rude that sounded. 'I'm sorry, Granddad! It's just that you've done so much for me and it's strange . . .'

'I know, love,' he said, putting his arms around her as she started to cry. 'I know. I'm sorry.'

Jade's birthday was on Sunday, the second of August.

'All I really want for my birthday,' Jade had said during lunch to Becca and Laura about a fortnight before, 'is to be ready for the One Day Event.' While Pip's hooves had recovered, the paddocks were still so sludgy that practising jumping and dressage was out of the question.

'I've got some news you might like, then,' Becca said. 'Mum and Dad have made a dressage arena in the back paddock.'

This did cheer Jade up. Although the test for

the pre-training pony class was simple and didn't involve anything she couldn't already do on Pip, she still felt butterflies in her stomach when she thought about competing.

'Could we come over and practise if it's fine next weekend?'

'Of course! I want you to. It's way easier practising with someone else than alone.'

'Am I going to have to get a pony?' Laura said suddenly, in an odd voice.

'That'd be great,' Jade said.

'No,' Becca said, seeing that Laura was upset. 'Don't be silly.'

Laura was frowning. 'All you ever talk about is riding — there's only so much fun someone can have watching from the fence line.'

'I'm sorry, Laura!' Jade said. 'You're right: we've got one-track minds.'

'I love horses too, but I just wish we could talk about something else sometimes. Whenever you say, "I hope it's fine in the weekend so I can ride," I think, "I hope it's wet in the weekend so they'll come over and watch a DVD."'

It was wet that weekend, and they did watch a DVD. They also spent some time planning Jade's party for the following weekend. All Laura's talk of cakes and candles and presents irritated Jade, though — it still didn't feel right to celebrate.

'Look,' Jade said quietly, as Laura wrote a list of Jade's favourite foods, 'I'm sorry, but I don't think I want a party at all.'

'You have to — it's your birthday,' Laura insisted. 'Your mum would want you to.'

'How would you know that?' Jade shouted.

'I'm sorry, Jade!' Laura called as Jade left the living room, slamming the door.

There was no more talk of parties the following week at school. And the sun had finally come out again, so Jade was happy. She even managed to do a little jumping practice on Wednesday afternoon.

'If it's fine on Sunday, could we use your dressage arena?' Jade asked Becca, when Laura wasn't listening, 'as a sort of birthday present.'

'Um,' Becca said. 'Me and mum will be out, running errands.'

'Errands?' Jade said suspiciously.

When she woke on Sunday morning, her granddad was frying bacon and eggs for a birthday treat.

'Hope you don't mind,' he said. 'I had to do something special, and I'm partial to a cooked breakfast.'

Jade laughed. 'Thanks, Granddad. It's perfect.'

'Don't clean up!' Granddad said, when Jade had finished and went to the sink. 'You'll be wanting to go for a ride, I suppose?'

'You know me well,' she said.

'It's quite a long walk to the Whites', isn't it,' he said cryptically, as Jade put on her boots.

'Yeah, but I'm used to it now.'

'Well, if you want to make the journey quicker, have a look in the shed.'

Curious, Jade went out and opened the roller door. There in front of her was an old Raleigh bike with a white leather seat and a red frame, and a red helmet hanging over the handlebars. Although it was second-hand, it had obviously been beautifully restored by someone who knew what they were doing.

'Granddad! It's perfect! Thank you,' Jade said, kissing him on the cheek.

'You're welcome, girl. If you take it to school, you'll have time to ride Pip in the afternoons now.'

It was a much quicker journey to the Whites' that morning.

'Nice wheels,' Mr White said, as she rode in.

'Thanks. Granddad gave it to me for my birthday.'

'Your birthday? That's right! Many happy returns. As a birthday treat, shall we do some cross-country jumping?'

'I'd love to, but where?'

'Have a look at the back paddock — have you really not noticed before?'

Jade squinted down past Brandy and Hamlet. She saw a couple of old logs, but nothing else.

'You mean those logs?'

Mr White laughed. 'Saddle up and meet me down there.'

When Jade rode down, she saw not only old logs, but an impressive ditch and a reinforced bank, similar to the one at the pony club grounds.

'It's only small, but it should give you a taste. I built this when Abby was one-day-eventing.'

It was as if Pip knew it was Jade's birthday and wanted to please her. She was brave and clever, jumping the logs and clearing the ditch like she'd been doing it all her life.

'Do you think she's done this before?' Jade asked, patting Pip's sweaty neck as they walked back to the yards.

'I'd be surprised if she hadn't,' Mr White said. 'I do wonder how old she is; it's so hard to tell.'

Once Pip had been fed, watered and put back in the paddock, Mr White suggested that Jade come in for a birthday cup of tea with him and Mrs White.

'OK,' Jade said. 'But please don't try to give me a present — everything you've done for me since I arrived has been the best gift ever. I really am very grateful.'

'Don't go getting soppy on me,' Mr White said. 'It's just a cup of tea and maybe a piece of cake.'

When Jade walked into the kitchen and found not only Mrs White, but Laura, Becca and a young woman sitting around a table covered with baking, she couldn't be angry.

'Surprise!' Laura yelled.

'I know you didn't want a party, so this is more of a morning tea,' Mrs White said innocently.

'Thanks, everyone. This is lovely,' Jade said, sitting down next to the unfamiliar girl.

'Jade, this is Abby,' Mrs White said, and the unfamiliar girl shook Jade's hand.

'It's nice to finally meet you,' Abby said. 'I've heard that you're making good use of my hand-me-downs.'

'Yes, thanks,' Jade said shyly.

'I've got you a little present,' Abby said, passing Jade a parcel.

'You really shouldn't have — your parents have given me heaps already.'

'I know, I know. Just open it.'

Jade unwrapped the paper and found a slightly faded but spotless pale blue sweatshirt with FLAXTON PONY CLUB across the front and a small horseshoe motif at either end of the text.

'See — it's just another boring hand-me-down.' Abby said.

'No, it's better than that!' Jade said, delighted. 'I won't stand out like a sore thumb in my red jersey any more. Do riders wear their pony club sweatshirts to the One Day Event?' Jade asked hopefully.

'Yes, they do,' Abby said, smiling.

Laura and Becca had a gift for Jade, too. 'Well, more for Pip really,' Becca said, handing over another parcel.

Jade opened it eagerly and found a pair of elegant black tendon boots.

'Those'll be great in summer, when you're jumping Pip on harder ground,' Abby said.

'Does all this make you want to go out for a

ride, Abby?' Mr White asked, pouring himself a cup of tea.

'Maybe tomorrow,' Abby said. 'If Jade's free after school, we could go for a ride together.'

Jade had to admit that she'd enjoyed her little party, and couldn't have wished for better presents. That night in bed she wore her new sweatshirt while she read the Pony Club manuals that Mr White had loaned her, skipping ahead to the B-Certificate section just to see how far she still had to go.

The following wintry weeks were filled with cleaning — muddy boots, muddy ponies, muddy paddocks — and practising. Both Jade and Becca had memorized and become proficient at their dressage test and were now enjoying jumping at the fortnightly pony club rallies, gradually testing out the course they'd have to do for the One Day Event. They were even clearing some of the fences Jade had watched Ryan and Amanda jumping on her first day at pony club.

'I wish Amanda would fall off for once,' Becca

said, as they watched the intermediate group cantering around the grounds. 'I know that sounds horrible, but she's just so good, and she knows it.'

Jade laughed. 'I felt just like that when I met her on my first day here. Is she friends with Ryan?'

'Yeah, they've been competing against each other for years. I think he's got a crush on her.'

It was Becca's turn to jump the tyres, so the girls stopped chatting. For some reason — perhaps he'd seen a golfer in amongst the trees on the course next to the pony club — Dusty baulked at the fence, leaving Becca to slide over his head and land on the other side.

'Oh dear!' said a mean voice. 'It wasn't even a real jump either.'

Jade looked round and saw Ryan and Amanda trotting past, laughing.

'Are you going to let her talk like that about your cousin?' Jade said, looking Ryan straight in the eye.

'Yes, of course,' he said, laughing.

Amanda laughed, too. Then, casting an imperious eye over Jade, said, 'Love your new sweatshirt, Jade. But it's not quite new, is it?'

'You two! Get back over here!' their instructor yelled.

'Nice to talk,' Ryan said, 'but we've got some proper jumping to do, and an Olympian's instructing us.'

'Is that Jade?' their instructor called, coming over. Ryan and Amanda looked shocked.

'Hi, Michaela,' Jade said, beaming. 'This is my friend Becca.' She pointed to Becca, who'd remounted and just cleared the tyre fence without any problem.

'Good to see you here. I usually teach show-jumping, but with the ODE coming up, the kids wanted to practise their cross-country,' Michaela said, gesturing at Ryan and Amanda. 'You two, we'd better get back to it. The rest of the group is waiting. Good luck at the ODE, Jade.'

When they'd gone, Jade and Becca couldn't stop laughing.

'That was better than seeing Amanda fall off, wasn't it?' Jade asked. Becca agreed.

# Ribbons

September the sixth: the day of the One Day Event and also Father's Day. Jade had remembered to post a card to her father earlier that week. In it, she'd told him about how hard she'd been training with Pip. She said that she missed him and hoped he was all right. However, on the crisp Sunday morning, she tried not to think about him at all as she clumsily plaited Pip's long black mane. While Abby White had been home, she'd taught Jade how to divide the mane into fourteen little pigtails, fasten them with tiny black rubber bands, and then how to plait and roll up each section into a neat bun. Abby had made it look easy, but now she was back at university, and Jade was alone, cold and nervous, and making a mess of it.

In the end Mr White had a try, but his attempts weren't much better.

'One Day Events aren't judged on appearances,' he consoled. 'So long as you ride well, you'll be in with a chance.'

However, Becca's mum disagreed: when Jade rode Pip over to where Dusty was tied up at the truck, she insisted on fixing the plaits. In less than five minutes, and with a few deft movements involving a needle, black thread and some hair-spray, she'd transformed Pip from dishevelled to chic.

The first event was the dressage. The girls collected their numbers and walked and trotted in circles to keep calm.

Becca went first and rode well.

'You could have loosened up a bit, dear — you were clearly nervous — but at this level it's better to be stiff and controlled than relaxed and all over the place. Don't you agree, Jim?' Becca's mum asked Mr White, who'd come over with a deck chair and a bottle of water mixed with lime cordial.

'Yes. I think you did a fine job, Becca. Stop fretting, Jade!'

Jade was walking Pip in a tight figure of eight, pulling nervously at her mouth, despite the pony already being on the bit.

'Sorry, I'm just—'

'I know, nervous. No time to be nervous, though, you're next after this girl.'

Jade rode slowly around the ring, pleased that Pip's ears were pricked. *It's just dressage*, she thought to herself. *Nothing to be afraid of. It's not like I'm going to fall off or embarrass myself. And it's not the end of the world if it isn't perfect.* Jade didn't quite manage to convince herself of this, however.

She was almost relaxed as Pip trotted into the arena and up the centre line. She remembered to halt halfway and salute the judge. *I think that was a square halt*, Jade thought, remembering not to look down or make too many encouraging noises to Pip.

Trotting in 20-metre circles and doing an extended walk in a diagonal line were a piece of cake for Pip, who seemed to be taking the ceremony in her stride. As they finished and left the arena, Jade heard clapping. It was only Mr White, Becca and Becca's mum, but it still felt nice.

'How was it?' Jade asked, dismounting and loosening the girth.

'Not bad. Not bad at all,' Mr White said. 'Pip was a touch sluggish to begin with, but it was a very competent performance.'

Not wanting to be too full for the cross-country, Becca and Jade shared a punnet of chips for lunch while Dusty and Pip rested beside Becca's truck.

The cross-country course was small, but included a range of jumps — ditches, logs, the Helsinki steps; smaller versions of all the pre-intermediate jumps, except the water.

Becca went first again. She was terribly nervous

and Dusty picked up on it. In the starting box he did a little rear, which didn't make her feel any better. At the first jump, a friendly log, he refused. This was simple naughtiness that Becca wasn't going to stand for. She tapped him gently behind her leg with her whip, pointed him at the jump again and flew over. After that initial hiccup, both pony and rider performed beautifully, cantering up hill and down dale as if they'd been doing it much longer than a few months.

'Shame about the beginning, Becca, because otherwise that was a first-class round,' Mr White said. 'You rode masterfully.'

'Thanks. I was just so nervous at the start. I feel like doing it again now, though,' Becca said, flushed from her ride.

'Well, you can't. It's my turn now,' Jade said, grimly trying to ignore the butterflies in her stomach. A small girl called Lana Stewart had just been eliminated for a fall at the tricky in-and-out. She was fine, but it seemed like a bad omen to Jade.

However, once she and Pip had left the starting

box it was no longer a competition with people watching so much as a canter around a paddock filled with fun obstacles. The only one that Pip looked like refusing was the Helsinki steps — three steep banks in a row like a staircase. But, with a click of her tongue and a press of the legs, Jade encouraged her pony and scrambled up the jump satisfactorily.

'That was fantastic!' she said after she'd cantered through the finish flags, slowed down in a circle, then walked back to the others.

'Pip looked like she was enjoying herself too,' Becca said.

There wasn't a long wait before the showjumping, just time to give the horses a drink and a quick rest.

Although the show-jumps weren't more than 70 centimetres high, the course was twisty and some earlier riders had come to grief. Becca and Jade had walked the course, noting the number of strides between the double and the relatively tight turn they'd need to take between fences eight and nine.

'No one has had a clear round yet, apparently,' Mr White warned, as Becca warmed up over the practice fence.

'I probably won't either,' Becca said, despondently.

'Not with that attitude!' Becca's mum said. 'Just ride sensibly — don't go too fast, remember the course. You'll be fine.'

Dusty had learnt to be a clever little showjumper during his time with the McAlpines, so Becca really didn't have to worry. Her nerves meant that she got a couple of strides wrong and ended up on his neck at one point, but competitive Dusty would settle for nothing less than a clear round.

'I didn't deserve that; he did everything,' Becca said gratefully, jumping out of the saddle with a sigh of relief. 'He's been great today.'

'I hope Pip's just as good,' Jade said, enviously. She knew Pip was a bit too big for this course, but she also knew that if she did what Michaela had told her — kept her horse slow and calm so that she could judge the strides correctly — a clear round was possible.

'Good luck, Jade,' Mr White called as she entered the ring, but Jade didn't hear: she was completely focused on the course.

The first jump, a low red-and-white oxer, was fine and Pip cleared it easily. But as they turned towards the second jump, a blue straight-bar, a dog barked, upsetting Pip. She cantered too fast and Jade had to sit right back and hold her until the last moment. It wasn't an elegant leap, but they got over clear. The rest of the course was manageable until the double, which was slightly too short for Pip's long legs. Again, Jade held her back, trying to keep her stride short but still full of impulsion. Pip's hind hooves touched the pole in the second jump of the double, but nothing fell. Now there was just the tricky turn from jumps eight to nine. Jade made sure Pip was on the right leg as she turned, and leaned out slightly, to keep her horse balanced. It worked: they approached the last jump perfectly and Pip cleared it.

'Was that clear?' Jade asked Mr White as she dismounted.

'Yes, it was. You were a bit lucky that 7B didn't fall though.'

'It wasn't luck at all!' Becca's mum said. 'That was a really nicely ridden round. You're going to be in a good position for a ribbon, Jade.'

Before any ribbons were awarded, there was still the pre-intermediate pony showjumping to go. Jade and Becca unsaddled, washed and fed their well-behaved steeds, before buying a couple of steak sandwiches from the food caravan and going back to watch Ryan's and Amanda's rounds.

Ryan did a fast, showy clear round, which Mr White said should have been slower. Amanda, riding in the same style, didn't fare so well. At the tight corner, her bay mare overbalanced and slipped right over, with Amanda underneath her.

'Oh, no!' Becca said sincerely, as they watched Amanda's mother and someone from St John's run across the ring to her. 'I feel awful now.'

'Why?' Becca's mother said. 'That wasn't your fault.'

'No, it's just, well, a couple of weeks ago I said I'd love to see her fall off.'

'That'll teach you for being nasty,' Becca's mum said. 'Don't worry, it looks like they're both standing up now. No broken bones.'

It was nearly five o'clock and the sun was setting as the prize-giving began. The Pony Club District Commissioner, none other than Mrs Thompson, the D-Certificate examiner, distributed pre-training pony prizes first.

'In fourth place, we have number nine: Theresa Hopkins on Rose Red.' A small freckly girl in a turquoise sweatshirt came up to collect her green ribbon and her prize, a bottle of hoof oil.

'In third place is number five: Jacqueline Kelly on Lancelot.' A tall girl with blonde plaits shook Mrs Thompson's hand and accepted the yellow ribbon and a small grooming kit.

'In second place is number six: Rebecca Brown

on Gold Dust.' Becca, blushing, stepped forward and took the blue ribbon and a year's subscription to *Horse and Pony*.

'Well done, darling!' Becca's mum whispered, hugging her daughter as she came back.

'And finally, in first place, we have number seven: Jade Lennox on Pip.'

Jade honestly hadn't thought about ribbons, let alone red ones — she'd been happy just to get around the cross-country course without falling off and to have a clear round in the showjumping. Mrs Thompson handed her the red ribbon and a beautiful red travel rug.

Jade thought she couldn't be happier until a voice from the crowd shouted, 'Her name's not Pip — it's Onyx. And she's not yours!'

Suddenly it felt like everyone was looking at Jade, especially the short, stocky woman who'd spoken.

'Come on, Jade,' Mr White said. 'Let's talk about this away from the prize-giving.'

Becca looked at Jade sympathetically as she left, but most people were staring at her with disgust.

Ryan was smirking, and, as she passed him, he muttered, 'I can't believe you actually stole a horse.'

'I didn't steal her!' Jade shouted. 'I saved her from the pound.'

'Shh, Jade. Come on,' Mr White said.

Outside the pony club shed, the stocky woman was looking pleased with herself.

'That's my horse you're riding,' she said.

'I'm sorry,' Jade said. 'I didn't know.'

'Didn't stop to wonder who you were stealing from when you took her?' The woman was enjoying the fight.

'I knew I was taking her from the pound. In fact, the pound know I have her.' Mr White had his hand on Jade's shoulder, which gave her some confidence.

'Well, she's still mine,' the woman said. 'And I want her back.'

'How long ago did she go missing from your paddock?' Mr White asked.

'About a year ago. I never thought I'd see her

again — and then today she wins a pony club One Day Event! I only came along to drive the truck for my niece. Lucky there's room in it for an extra horse.'

'You can't take her,' Jade said in a small voice, knowing that the stocky woman probably could.

'Do you have her papers? Did you buy her?' the woman asked nastily. 'No, so I think you'll find that I can take her. Actually, I already have.'

'What!' Mr White exclaimed. Jade was already running back to the horse-float. Pip had gone.

When she ran back to where Mr White and the stocky woman were standing, Jade yelled, 'Where's your truck? Just let me say goodbye to her.'

'I'm not going to encourage a thief like you,' the stocky woman hissed. Jade started to defend herself, but the woman cut her off. 'I don't want to hear any excuses about the pound. You've taken what isn't yours and that's theft in my book.'

'Would you at least consider letting me buy Pip, I mean, Onyx?' Mr White said, trying to restrain his frustration.

'I'll think about it,' the woman said. 'But you

realize that a good pony like that is worth a high price.'

At this, Mr White finally lost his temper. 'We've spent the last six months turning her into the pony she is — with my feed, and Jade's riding. This is ridiculous! Why should we even believe that she's yours? I want to see papers before you take our pony anywhere.'

The woman looked furious. 'Of course I don't have her papers on me. I don't carry them everywhere I go. If you want to buy Onyx, you can call this number.' Pausing, the woman scribbled her name and a phone number on a piece of paper from her bag and passed it to Mr White. 'And that's the end of the matter for now!'

Jade and Mr White followed the woman to a huge old truck covered in peeling yellow paint, but they couldn't see Pip.

'Don't bother — I've already loaded the horses,' the woman sneered, hopping into the driver's seat, next to a teenage girl. They drove off.

That night, Jade wouldn't eat dinner. She grabbed her pyjamas from her bedroom, then went to the bathroom and stood under the steaming shower for about half an hour, sobbing.

When she finally emerged, bright red from the hot water, and returned to her bedroom, she found a plate of cheese and Marmite sandwiches and a lukewarm cup of tea on her bedside table. Grateful that her granddad hadn't tried to talk to her, Jade sipped at the tea, then nibbled on one sandwich and soon finished the plate. She fell asleep sad, but at least not hungry.

First thing the next morning, Mr White phoned the number on the crumpled piece of paper.

'Is that Val?' he asked, when a woman answered.

'Yes?' Her voice sounded sleepy, as if she wasn't used to early mornings.

'This is Jim White. I've been grazing your horse, Onyx, for the past six months and I'd like him back.'

'Oh, it's you. Well, I'm sure we can make some

sort of an arrangement. Sorry about all the drama yesterday — I was just so surprised to see my horse.'

'Would you have time for a visit today? I'll bring my horse-float and cheque book.'

'Certainly. I'll be asking $4,000.' Val gave Mr White her address.

Jade was still lying in bed, reading *My Friend Flicka* for the fourteenth time, when Mr White arrived at her granddad's house.

'Jade, get up, it's nearly eleven!' Mr White called from the hallway.

Shocked, Jade leapt out of bed, hurriedly pulled on jeans and a T-shirt and opened her door. 'What are you doing here?' she asked.

'We're getting Pip back. Out to the ute now!'

Jade didn't need to be told twice. After pulling on odd socks and her boots, she ran out to the driveway.

Pip trotted over to the fence line and neighed when the familiar ute and horse-float drove up Val's driveway. Val soon emerged from the house, in Ugg boots and a polar-fleece vest.

'Hi, guys,' she said, much friendlier than yesterday. Jade stared at her stonily.

'Do you have the papers?' Mr White said, cutting to the chase.

'Right here,' she said, fishing a folded A4 sheet of paper out of her pocket.

Mr White pulled a pair of spectacles out of his pocket and unfolded the paper. 'This says that she's 14.2. How did you manage that?'

'Oh, I didn't get her registered — Mum did,' Val said. 'Nyx was my little sister Tessa's pony. I wasn't interested in riding at that stage, not like Tess; she loved all the competitions — jumping and that. You should've seen the fuss her and Mum went to make Nyx eligible for pony classes. They took her shoes off and filed her hooves right down. I think they even had an icepack on her withers at the measuring booth.'

'What happened to Tessa?' Jade asked, curiosity

overcoming her dislike of this woman.

'Well, Tess crashed her car' — Jade flinched slightly, but Val didn't notice — 'and couldn't ride anymore. She wanted Nyx to stay in the family and I inherited her, despite being too old for pony club. So I started Western riding.'

'How long did you ride Pip, I mean, Onyx?' Jade asked.

'A few years,' Val said.

'I saw her at the pound back in January. I asked the pound if I could keep her and they said yes. Since then I've been riding her and taking care of her,' Jade said slowly.

'I can see that. And I suppose I believe that you didn't steal her. I mean, look at you, you're so young.'

'Much, much younger than Pip,' Mr White cut in, still scrutinizing the registration papers.

'What?' Jade asked. 'How old's Pip?'

'Twenty-three!'

Jade gasped. Val looked uncomfortable. 'Yeah, I was going to mention that.'

# Horses and ponies

Having found out Pip's real age, Mr White would pay no more than $500 for Val's Onyx.

'But she's been performing like a horse half her age,' Val protested. 'That's what I tried to tell the others, but they wouldn't listen.'

'The others?' Jade asked.

'Well, when Tess died I thought I could find Nyx a better home. A pony club home, like yours.'

On the way home, with Pip in the float and her registration papers in the glove box, Jade alternated between awkwardly thanking Mr White for buying back her pony and seething over Val.

'What a repulsive woman!' Jade exclaimed for the third time, as the ute pulled into the Whites' driveway. 'Trying to sell her dead sister's pony. And filing poor Pip's feet just for a stupid piece of paper.'

'There was certainly something a bit odd about her,' Mr White agreed. 'I wouldn't be surprised if she'd given Pip to the pound herself. But the main thing is that Pip is home. And this pony registration will come in handy, what with show season approaching. You might call it a stupid piece of paper now, but you'll probably be grateful for it when you're competing at the Flaxton Show.'

Jade sat quietly, wanting to say she didn't really care about the show: if she'd been Tessa, she would never have put Pip through the ordeal of being shrunk. She'd be just as happy going for long road rides. That would have been a lie, though. Jade felt uncomfortably selfish. Perhaps she didn't deserve the big black pony that was now hers?

Parking the ute, Mr White leant across and got the registration out of the glove box. Looking at it again, he started to chuckle.

'What's funny?' Jade asked.

'Nothing much — it's just that Jade and Onyx are both gemstones. You make quite a pair.'

Since finding out Pip's real age, Jade had been riding her cautiously. Mr Finch had come around the following week and put a shiny new set of shoes on Pip, so that she'd have enough grip and support for jumping. The tendon boots that Becca and Laura had given Jade for her birthday were good to use as well. Pip seemed to like them, too: whenever Jade did up the velcro straps, Pip knew that the ride would include jumping practice or a good gallop.

In preparation for the C-Certificate exam, Jade was learning to trust Pip enough to let her go at full speed. The first time they practised this in the large paddock, with Mr White watching,

Jade was worried that once she got Pip going she wouldn't be able to stop her.

'You'll be fine, Jade,' Mr White said with characteristic optimism. 'Just keep your legs on firmly, lean forward and grab a handful of mane. When you want to stop, lean back gradually, sit deep in the saddle and begin to pull Pip in a circle — but not too sharply mind; you don't want her slipping over.'

This advice, while wise, was unnecessary. Pip behaved like a lady, responding to Jade's aids and extending into a gallop, then relaxing back to a canter, then a trot when asked.

'I sometimes wonder if she's too good for me,' Jade said, grinning and patting her neck. 'I won't know what to do when I ride a difficult horse.'

Mr White looked thoughtful. 'I'd hardly call him difficult, but Hamlet would be a change of gear. Would you like to try him next time?'

'I'd love to,' Jade said, flattered that Mr White would let her ride his horse. 'Isn't he too big for me, though?'

'To be honest, Pip's a bit big for you too, Jade,

but you manage fine on her. I'm not suggesting that you gallop and jump Hamlet — he's not much of a jumper really, anyway. Doing a bit of schooling on him would give you an idea of how a different horse moves and has different habits. It might be worth getting Becca around here one weekend and swapping ponies with her. I imagine Dusty would prove a bit more difficult than Pip.'

The next day at school, Jade suggested the swap to Becca, who thought it was a great idea.

'It's funny you should say that,' Becca said, 'because I was talking to Ryan about the C-Certificate exam, and he told me that when he sat it the examiner made them swap ponies.'

'Well, that settles it,' Jade said. 'This Saturday, you'll ride Pip and I'll ride Dusty, and maybe we'll both have a go on Hamlet.'

'Seeing as everyone seems to be swapping ponies,' Laura said, 'do you think I could come along and have a little ride, too?'

Jade and Becca were surprised — Laura had never wanted to ride before. 'Of course, Laura!' Becca said. 'We've been hoping you'd ride with us for ages.'

In the first real sunshine Flaxton had seen in months, Jade biked to the Whites' early on Saturday morning. It felt like spring as she caught not just Pip, but Brandy and Hamlet too, and brought them into the yards.

Beginning with Pip, she groomed each horse until her arms ached and she was covered in horse hair. By nine-thirty, when Mr White came out of the house, there were tumbleweeds of the horses' winter coats rolling about in the yards.

'You've been busy!' he said to Jade through a cloud of dust and Hamlet's dark brown hair. 'They look much smarter now.' Pip, in particular, had patches of sleek, black summer coat showing beneath the softer winter fur.

'I'm exhausted!' Jade said, having finally finished. 'Hamlet's just like a big teddy bear.'

Laura arrived next, and, with the help of Mr White, was soon in Brandy's saddle.

'Are you sure my stirrups are the right length?' she asked, looking down at her feet. 'My legs feel funny. And it's quite high up, isn't it?'

Jade giggled. 'You'll get used to it. You look alright, if that's any consolation.'

'Jade's right,' Mr White said. 'You've got a very good seat and you're keeping your hands stiller than most beginners manage to.'

'I think it's from spending so many weekends watching and listening to the others,' Laura said. 'It's like I've been learning to ride too, except without ever hopping on a horse.'

Becca and her mum drove up the driveway as Mr White began leading Brandy slowly around the paddock.

'It mightn't be such a good day for swapping,' Becca said tetchily as she led Dusty out of the horse-truck. 'This here is one naughty pony.'

Becca's mum explained that Becca had spent the past hour trying to catch Dusty, who'd run circles around her.

'It's all that spring grass,' Becca's mum said. 'Is Pip the same?'

As if on cue, Pip opened her mouth and had a big yawn. Jade laughed. 'No, she's still calm as can be, aren't you, old lady?' she said, scratching Pip behind the ear.

Around the other ponies, Dusty was slightly better behaved, but from the moment Jade mounted him she knew he was very different to Pip.

'How are you doing, Jade?' Mr White asked. 'Keep your heels down and your legs on. He's got his back up.'

'Is that what it is,' Jade asked shakily. 'He feels all wrong — like a jack-in-the-box that's about to leap up.'

'He might leap up, Jade,' Becca's mum said, 'so be careful.'

Focusing entirely on keeping Dusty calm, Jade found that, after half an hour of just walking and trotting in circles, she was tired out. However, the hard work paid off, and Dusty began to listen to Jade's commands.

'You ready for a canter now, boy?' Jade asked. 'You won't get excited and buck me off?'

Very subtly, Jade gathered up her reins, sat back in the saddle and pressed with her inside leg, and Dusty sprang into a bouncy canter.

'I think he's ready for a wee jump,' Jade said, pleased.

'Go for it,' Becca said, riding Pip out of Jade's way as she and Dusty approached the smallest straight-bar. Dusty picked up his knees and popped over neatly.

'I can't let Pip watch from the sidelines,' Becca said, urging her into a canter and pointing her at the straight-bar too. Slightly lazier than Dusty, Pip knocked the rail off. Not wanting to finish on a bad note, Becca brought Pip around for another go, this time concentrating on slowing her down and getting more scope in her stride. It worked — Pip cleared the jump well.

'Who'd like to try Hamlet now?' Mr White asked, as the girls hopped off the ponies. 'Laura?'

Laura laughed. 'No, thanks. I think I'm all horsed out for today.'

'Becca?'

'Yes, please. I've never been on a horse before.'

'Hamlet will have quite a different gait and temperament to Dusty,' Mr White said. 'That might take a bit of getting used to, but he's a gentleman really.'

While Becca schooled Hamlet, adjusting well to his longer stride, Jade rubbed down both ponies and gave them some hay. When it came to her turn to try Hamlet, she was utterly exhausted, but couldn't resist.

Once she was up in the saddle, looking down from what seemed a great height, Jade got her second wind. After half an hour, Mr White made her stop.

'Hamlet's not used to all this attention. He's an old man, too — nearly as old as Pip. That's probably enough for today.'

After the swap, Becca and Jade agreed that each horse they'd ridden had its faults and strengths.

'It was lovely not having my arms pulled out of their sockets, and being able to concentrate on getting Pip to go on the bit,' Becca said. 'But she was more sluggish than Dusty, and not as clever at jumping. No offence.'

'None taken,' Jade said. 'I felt the same. Dusty was full of get-up-and-go and really fun to jump, but he wasn't as predictable as Pip. And Hamlet was another story altogether.'

'I loved riding Hamlet,' Becca gushed. 'His strides, especially the canter, were so smooth and elegant. I can't wait to have a horse one day.'

It wasn't long before Becca got to ride a horse again. The following weekend, during the C-Certificate examination, Mrs Thompson asked all the candidates to swap mounts, just as Ryan had said she would.

Becca and Jade looked at each other excitedly, but Mrs Thompson saw this and made sure that they swapped with other riders.

Becca had to give Dusty to a tall boy with nervous hazel eyes, whose horse was a 15.2-hand skewbald gelding. Pip went to a girl whom Jade had seen somewhere before. As soon as she'd had a better look at the girl's wild-eyed roan mare, Jade knew where — at Michaela Lewis's. It was Kristen's friend Andy.

Having completed the theoretical part of the exam, and jumped and galloped on their own mounts, the swap was the last test.

'Everyone walking in a circle around me, please, as if you were in a ring class. When I tell you, please trot and canter.'

Jade knew she'd have her work cut out as soon as she mounted Piper, the roan. *I'm so glad I practised on Dusty*, Jade thought, as she did her best to make her aids clear but gentle. The roan had been playing up for her rider throughout the exam — not bucking or rearing, but consistently pulling at the bit, throwing her head up and bending inside out around corners. Andy must have had experience dealing with these flaws because, although she held Piper very tightly, she seldom let her pony put a foot wrong.

'Trot, please,' Mrs Thompson said. Everybody shortened their reins and gave the correct aids. Jade longed to look over and see how the others were doing with their strange mounts, but she had to keep concentrating. All she could see was Pip in front of her, going nicely for Andy.

'And canter!' Mrs Thompson called, satisfied with their trotting.

At Jade's command to canter, Piper gave an enormous buck and rushed forward. If Jade hadn't been cautious and gripping tightly with her legs, she would've been thrown over the naughty pony's head. Instead, she sat back and managed to pull Piper in a circle so that she didn't run into the back of Pip. Ignoring the examiner now, she kept circling Piper until she calmed down, and then waited until she'd brought her back to a walk before entering the circle again.

Mrs Thompson called the riders into the centre.

'I'm sorry about that,' Jade said guiltily.

'No,' Mrs Thompson said, 'you did the right thing. That pony's just full of beans — or else she has a sore back. Does she often do this?' Mrs Thompson asked Andy.

Andy blushed. 'Unfortunately, yes. I've had her for the last six months and she's bucked nearly every time I've ridden her.'

'Have you had the vet come and look at her?'
Mrs Thompson asked.

'No,' Andy blushed again.

'Give him a call. It's probably something more
than naughtiness if she does it so regularly.'

At the end of the exam, every rider was given
their C Certificate, although the tall boy with the
nervous eyes was told he'd 'just scraped through
by the skin of his teeth' and 'should practise
keeping his hands still'.

When everyone had swapped back to their own
pony, Jade, Becca and Andy rode over to the horse-
floats together.

'Dusty's a bit of a handful,' Becca said, 'but
nothing compared with Piper.'

'Thanks,' Andy said, ironically.

'Sorry, I didn't mean it like that. What I meant
is, you must be a very good rider to deal with that
every day.'

'I felt like a good rider when I had Snapdragon,'

Andy said sadly. 'He was only 13.2, but we often won competitions jumping 1 metre. I grew out of him, though, and now I'm stuck with you, aren't I, beautiful?' Andy said, stroking Piper's stiff neck. 'She's only four, so hopefully there's still time to get her out of this bad habit. I really hope she's not injured.'

'How was the skewbald horse?' Jade asked Becca.

'Fat and uncomfortable,' Becca replied, making the girls laugh. 'It's true!' She giggled. 'He didn't do anything wrong, but just had a weird stride and I felt like I was sitting on an oil drum.'

'Pip was lovely,' Andy said to Jade. 'So much more polite than my monster.'

'Yeah, polite's a good word for her,' Jade said. 'Andy, are you going to be showjumping Piper this season?'

'I hope so,' Andy replied. 'If I don't break my neck before the first show!'

'Well,' Jade said. 'Becca and I will be practising together, if you'd like to join us sometime. I mean, I know you're friends with Kristen Lewis and that her mum's jumps are amazing, but—'

'I'd love to!' Andy said. 'Kristen and I go to school together, but I don't really like riding with her. She's just so much better than me. Riding with you guys would be fun.'

'Thanks,' Jade said, imitating Andy's earlier tone.

'No!' Andy cried. 'You know what I mean!'

# Surprise!

*Wednesday, 2 December*

*Dear Dad,*
*The Wanford Sports Day went really well. Pip and*
*I got a first in the under-14 bending race, a third in*
*the under-14 paced and mannered class, a second*
*in the under-14 round the ring jumping, and a*
*fourth in the 1-metre showjumping. I've started*
*hanging my ribbons on the wall in my room. At*
*first Granddad wasn't happy about the drawing*
*pins in the new paint, but when he saw how much*
*better they made the room look, he came round.*

*I can't wait to see you at Christmas! Grand-dad's planning to cook a ham. He's getting more adventurous with his dinners, but I'm not sure if he's ready for ham! It'll be strange because it's been so long. I've grown about 4 centimetres taller — it's lucky Pip's big otherwise I might grow out of her soon. Anyway, I think it'll be a nice Christmas.*

*It's a shame you won't be here a week earlier. The 20th is the Flaxton Sports Day, which has a 1.10-metre showjumping class that Mr White thinks I should enter. Never mind; there will be lots of other chances for you to see me riding Pip.*

*Do you think the local paper will have a job for you in Flaxton? I hope so. I guess there isn't much that happens here, though, except horse shows.*

*See you in 23 sleeps!*
*Lots of love,*
*Jade*

The show season was finally in full swing, and Jade and Ryan had been told off twice for chatting about riding instead of working quietly in class.

Now that she had her C Certificate and had started winning ribbons, Ryan seemed more interested in Jade. And now that Ryan had stopped hanging around with Amanda at pony club, Jade found him less annoying. She'd almost forgiven him for his comment about horse-stealing, and it was nice to have someone in class who understood what she really wanted to be doing with her time, rather than learning about fractions.

'Give us a look,' Ryan whispered, pulling out the schedule for the Flaxton Sports Day from Jade's desk. He saw that the 1.10-metre showjumping event was circled.

'Are you entering this one?'

'Yeah. I think Pip's ready.'

'I got second in it last year.'

'Well done.'

'I'm planning to win it this year.'

'Ryan! Shh!' Mrs Crawford said, looking up from her desk.

'Your cousin is obsessed with winning,' Jade told Becca that weekend as they went for a road ride to cool down the ponies after a jumping session.

'I know,' Becca said. 'He's always been like that. I'm not nearly as competitive as him, but it would be nice to beat him one day.'

'Being competitive is good,' said Andy, who'd been practising with them. 'You have to be that way if you want to get to the top, like Kristen. But I think it's more important to just enjoy spending time with your pony and improving at your own pace.' She patted Piper's neck. 'Since the vet told me that Piper's back was OK, and that her bucking was most likely caused by being competed with too soon after she'd been broken in, I've tried to be really patient with her. I think we'll just enter the 80-centimetre showjumping at the Sports. There's no rush.'

The others nodded in approval.

'I feel kind of the same about Pip,' Jade said. 'Because she's so old, I don't want to push her too hard. But at the same time I know that when she's in the right mood she can still jump like a pony half her age. I'd rather not get placed in the show-jumping than injure her, though.'

'Dusty doesn't have any excuses,' Becca laughed. 'He's the perfect age and a clever jumper. I just hope it all goes well on the big day.'

The big day arrived in no time, which was good because it also marked the start of the summer holidays.

On the last Friday at school, as they packed up the desks in the classroom and then went to prize-giving, Jade could think of nothing but the course she would jump with Pip later that afternoon.

'I think it's you,' a girl said, nudging Jade as she daydreamed in the assembly hall.

'What?' Jade said, with a start.

'You've won the Year 7 Language prize,' the girl said impatiently. 'Quick!'

Jade got up from her seat and awkwardly walked to the front of the hall to accept the certificate from the school principal.

'Congratulations,' he said, shaking her hand.

'I hear you did an excellent job on an assignment about our local sporting hero.'

'Um, yeah,' Jade said, shyly, rushing back to her seat and blushing.

After another blissful ride with Pip, Jade biked home from Mr White's in the late afternoon sunlight, looking forward to showing her grand-dad the certificate. It wasn't as exciting to her as the C Certificate, but she knew he'd be pleased.

'Granddad!' she called, letting herself in the back door.

'Surprise!' called back a familiar voice from the kitchen.

'Dad?' Jade said, hardly believing that the father she hadn't seen for nearly a year was now standing in the kitchen drinking a cup of tea with her granddad.

He came over and enveloped her in a huge, tight hug. Jade could hardly breathe, but didn't mind. He smelt just the same as she remembered. And the cut on his head had healed now, leaving an impressive scar.

'You're right! You *have* grown taller,' he said, his eyes shining.

'How are you here so early?' Jade asked. 'I thought you weren't coming until Christmas.'

'You mentioned a horse show in your letter,' he said, grinning. 'I didn't want to miss that.'

Over a celebratory dinner of fish and chips, Jade brought her dad up-to-date on all that she'd left out of her letters.

'Michaela Lewis was so nice to me, Dad. And I wrote so much about her that I got an A$^+$ for my assignment. And this,' she said, remembering the certificate and pulling it out of her school bag.

'That's wonderful,' her dad said, holding it back to get a better look, as if it were a work of art.

'I think I like writing,' Jade said. 'Who knows? Maybe I'll become a journalist like you one day. After I've gone to the Olympics in the New Zealand showjumping team, of course.'

Her dad laughed, but then looked serious.

'Unfortunately, I'm not a journalist right now, Jade. That's something we'll have to talk about — but not now.'

'Why not now?' Jade asked. 'What's wrong?'

Jade's granddad screwed the fish and chip paper up into a ball and took it into the kitchen.

'I know you've got a life here now, Jade,' her dad said. 'That's wonderful; I'm so glad that you could adapt and make new friends. But I really don't think that there's work for me as a journalist here in Flaxton.'

'I can't go back to Auckland!' Jade cried, pre-empting her father.

'I know that you don't want to leave Pip,' her dad said, holding her hand.

'You're right,' she said. 'I don't! She's my responsibility now.'

'I know,' her dad said, wearily. 'I didn't want to talk about this now. Let's just try and enjoy ourselves until the New Year?'

Jade was silent, staring hard at the bottle of tomato sauce in front of her on the table.

'Will we really have to go back to Auckland next

year?' Jade said, trying to swallow the lump in her throat.

'Maybe. I'm sorry,' her dad said. 'I am trying my best to sort this out, though; I really am.'

The night before what felt like the biggest day of the year, when Jade most needed her sleep, she tossed and turned, anxiously wondering what would happen to Pip if she had to leave Flaxton.

When her alarm went off at five-thirty the next morning, Jade felt like she hadn't slept at all. Plaiting her hair tightly back and staring in the bathroom mirror, Jade thought her eyes looked puffy and horrible. *I'll never win the 1.10-metre jumping if I'm half-asleep*, she thought.

Pedalling to Mr White's through the crisp morning mist, Jade began to perk up. Just thinking about the jumping and imagining the tight turns she'd have to take in the jump-off — if she even got into the jump-off — made the adrenaline flow through her body.

Pip nuzzled Jade's arm as she groomed her.

'You're psychic, aren't you?' Jade said, miserably. 'You know I'm unhappy. I'm not going to tell you why, though — I don't want to make you unhappy, too.'

Becca's mum had arranged to bring the truck around to Mr White's at seven-thirty to take Jade and Pip to the show. Mr and Mrs White would follow at a more civilized hour, with Granddad and now Jade's father too.

'He's back already?' Becca asked excitedly, after Jade had told them about her dad's unexpectedly early arrival.

'Wow, I can't wait to meet him — I don't think I've ever known anyone who's been in prison before,' Becca said, without thinking.

'Rebecca!' Becca's mum scolded. 'Show a little sensitivity.'

'It's OK,' Jade said quietly. 'I'd probably be the same if it wasn't my dad.'

The sports grounds looked perfect when the truck rolled in to join the aisles of horse-floats in the loading area. Everywhere you looked there was greenish-yellow grass, riders wearing smart white numbers, and beautifully groomed horses.

Pip and Dusty weren't put to shame, though. Their riders had worked up a sweat making sure that their summer coats gleamed and that their tack was spotless.

'Dusty!' Becca shrieked, watching her mischievous pony take a large mouthful of grass just after she'd put on his bridle. A pale green trickle of chewed-up grass and saliva dribbled over the ring of Dusty's snaffle bit. As Becca tried to mop this off, another grassy dribble fell on the sleeve of her smart blue riding jacket. 'Mum! Dusty's filthy!'

Becca's mum just laughed and said callously, 'I told you to tie his lead rope more tightly.'

Careful to avoid staining her own black riding jacket — a slightly ill-fitting, but sufficiently smart, hand-me-down of Abby White's — Jade helped Becca clean up.

The riding and paced and mannered classes were first. In the warm-up area, they met Ryan,

Andy and a remote Amanda, who didn't bother to say hello.

'How's Piper behaving today?' Becca asked. 'She looks gorgeous.'

'Thanks,' Andy said. 'To be honest, she's a bit hyped-up, with all the other horses around. Not bucking, though, so that's something.'

Andy had spoken too soon. In the first event, the ten- to fourteen-year-olds' paced and mannered class, Piper's bucking commenced as soon as the judge commanded the riders to trot. Andy pulled her pony out of the circle and took her away to calm down.

Unfortunately, Pip had been spooked by Piper's bucking and was distracted for the rest of the event. Dusty, on the other hand, couldn't have looked better.

'Number twelve, number three, number two and number nineteen, please come in. Thank you to the rest of you,' the judge said.

Jade wasn't too disappointed as she walked to the sideline and halted next to Becca's mum.

'Becca's in second place,' Jade said happily.

'Yes,' said Becca's mum, 'but look who's in first place. He'll never let her hear the end of this.'

Jade looked and saw Ryan smirking as the red ribbon was tied around his pony's neck.

'Good effort,' he said patronizingly to Becca as they both rode over to Jade.

'Thanks,' Becca said with great restraint. 'You rode well, too.'

Ryan looked slightly disappointed that there was no argument, but not as disappointed as Amanda, who threw Becca a withering look.

Andy was back with a calmed-down Piper for the riding class. When Piper was good, she was very, very good, and Jade was delighted to see Andy called into the centre first. Another number was called soon after. It was Jade's!

'Well done,' Jade whispered, grinning at Andy as the ribbons were tied around their ponies' necks.

'I couldn't be more pleased,' Andy said, as they walked back to the floats to have a rest before the jumping. 'I don't usually like ring classes very much, but that was fun.'

Back at Becca's mum's truck, Jade found her fan club.

'Jolly good,' Mr White said, seeing that each rider had a ribbon. 'What a splendid start!'

# Showjumping

Mrs White had made a sumptuous picnic lunch, so after the ponies had been tied up, unsaddled and given some water, the girls sat down with the adults for some lime cordial, assorted club sandwiches, quiche, Cornish pasties, plums, apples, banana cake and Anzac biscuits.

'Usually I'm too nervous to eat before jumping,' Jade said, with her mouth full, 'but this food is *so* good.'

Mrs White looked pleased.

After everyone had eaten and drunk their fill, the girls and Ryan saddled up again and went with

Mr White to the showjumping practice arena.

'I hate it in here,' Andy said, stroking Piper's neck protectively. 'Everyone's going in different directions, and I always feel like I'm in the way of the big horses. Or someone's in front of me and they knock the pole down before I get a chance to jump the fence.'

Mr White laughed. 'Well, I'm here to help in that respect. I'll just stand in the middle, and if you want the jumps lowered or put up a few notches, say the word.'

As Jade cantered in circles and approached the practice fence, she could see, in her peripheral vision, her dad watching from the side. She was distracted and let Pip knock the rail down.

'Too flat,' Mr White said loudly. 'Collect her up, Jade. You can do better than that.'

He was right and Jade knew it. The next jump Pip did was perfect.

'Much better,' Mr White said.

Jade was concentrating so hard that she hadn't noticed Andy going into the ring for the 80-centimetre class.

'When did she walk the course?' Jade asked Becca, as they stopped and watched her round.

'Ages ago, while you were warming up,' Becca said, giggling. 'You're away with the fairies, aren't you?'

'I'm just tired,' Jade said. 'I didn't sleep well last night.'

Becca was going to ask why, but they stopped talking as the bell rang and Andy cantered Piper through the start flags.

Piper was accustomed to jumping much larger jumps than this, but was still easily distracted by the crowd and spooked by bright colours and strange shapes. She paused dramatically as she approached the white picket fence, but Andy skillfully encouraged her pony on and they managed to finish the course with a clear round.

More confident after the first round, Andy seemed to find the jump-off a piece of cake: she and Piper flew around in the winning time.

'You're cleaning up today,' Jade said, reaching over and patting Piper's neck as Andy pulled up beside them.

'She's been angelic. This is such a good note to end on.'

'Look at you!' said Kristen Lewis, who was walking past. 'Congratulations.'

'Thanks,' Andy said. 'It was only in the little jumping, but still, I have to start somewhere with her.'

'Are you riding today?' Jade asked Kristen.

'Yeah — I've got the pony grand prix later on,' Kristen said, as if it were nothing.

'Wow,' said Becca. 'Good luck!'

'Are you guys riding in the 1.10-metre class?' Kristen asked.

'Yeah,' Jade said, trying not to sound nervous.

'Cool, I'll go and get Mum. I reckon she'd like to see you riding.'

So, with the prospect of not just her dad and granddad watching, but Michaela Lewis too, Jade walked the 1.10-metre course grimly. The jumps looked bigger than the ones at home, and the course itself was so freshly painted and professional that Jade was already feeling guilty for knocking down the rails even though she and

Pip were yet to even enter the ring.

The double was, as usual, a little tight for Pip, Jade thought as she walked out the strides.

Ryan was the first of the three to do his round. Riding with characteristic flair, he went clear, but too fast.

'You were a bit lucky,' Mr White said. 'You don't need to race in the first round.'

'I don't need to, but I like to,' Ryan replied rudely.

Jade's number was called next. As she cantered in a circle, waiting for the starting bell, she saw Michaela, Mr White and Becca's mum standing at the fence line.

'I don't care if we don't win a ribbon,' Jade whispered to Pip. 'But if we get more than four faults, it'll be really embarrassing.'

Focusing like she never had before, Jade took all the advice she'd ever been given from Mr White, Becca's mum and Michaela and put it into practice. Approaching the first oxer calmly and on the right leg, Pip flew over and was ready for the turn on the brick wall. Slowing her pony down and collecting up her stride, Jade navigated Pip through the double without mishap and was ready with a click of the tongue to urge Pip over the picket fence. It was hardly necessary: by the tenth jump, Pip was in her element and leapt over perfectly to complete a clear round.

'Nice work,' Michaela said, as Jade rode out. 'You deserved that clear round. Really sensibly ridden.'

Inspired by Ryan and Jade, Becca was determined to join them in the jump-off.

'Is that Olivia McAlpine's pony?' Michaela asked Becca's mum, as Becca cleared the first jump elegantly.

'Yes, we bought Dusty from the McAlpines in April. He's been a bit of a handful as a first pony, but Becca's worked hard and it seems to have paid off.'

As if to prove her mum right, Becca expertly guided Dusty through the double.

'He's a neat wee jumper,' Kristen said,

approvingly. '1.10 metres is child's play for him. How old is he?'

'Only nine. So long as Becca doesn't outgrow him too soon, I think she could do quite well with him.'

'We're all in the jump-off!' Jade said excitedly, watching Becca canter through the finishing flags with a flourish.

'You might have your work cut out to get first place now, Ryan,' Becca's mum said, laughing.

'Hmm,' Ryan replied, looking serious.

The jump-off included the brick wall, the picket fence, the first oxer, the double, and the final straight-bar. It was a tight course, particularly the turn on to the double, but this didn't seem to discourage Ryan from trying to do it at a hundred miles an hour.

'He's going to come to grief if he carries on at that pace,' Mr White said, shaking his head.

'I can't watch,' Becca's mum said, turning away.

Just as they'd all predicted, the turn on to the

double was Ryan's downfall. Although he'd tried to sit back and balance his pony, they were still going far too fast and ended up smashing straight through the fence.

The clock was stopped as the fence was rebuilt, but Ryan's pony was holding his foreleg pathetically.

'Ryan!' Becca's mum shouted. 'Shady's cut his leg.'

Walking over to the fence, Ryan noticed that Shady was, indeed, very lame. He scratched him from the event and led his pony out of the ring, shamefaced.

'Well, that's that over,' he said quietly.

'What possessed you to go that fast?' Mr White said. 'I know it was a jump-off, but you're not stupid. Surely you knew he was bound to crash eventually?'

'I just wanted to win,' Ryan said, irritably.

'Now *that's* the way to win,' Michaela said, changing the subject as Jade and Pip began their jump-off.

Well aware that she was riding an old pony, and

a little shaken after watching Ryan's crash, Jade decided to play it safe. By keeping Pip at a collected canter, Jade was able to keep her turns on to each jump very tight. This method meant that she not only did a clear round, but she had a good time too.

'Super round,' Mr White said, patting Pip's neck. 'You're in with a great chance.'

'I don't know,' Jade said. 'It felt really slow.'

'For a big pony, you had her moving around that course very tightly,' Michaela said. 'I think you've got a good chance, too.'

Other than Ryan, Jade and Becca, there were four riders in the jump-off. Two of them dropped rails, and one was eliminated after three refusals at the brick wall.

'Well, we'll definitely get at least fourth,' Becca said, grinning, as she entered the ring. 'Third is fine with me.'

More relaxed now with this in mind, Becca's only care was to have fun with Dusty.

'She's motoring around!' Kristen said, impressed.

'But sensibly,' Mr White added. 'If only Ryan were here to see this.'

Ryan had gone back to the truck to clean Shady's leg and give him a feed. He returned just in time to hear the results called over the loudspeaker. Fourth place went to one of the girls who'd dropped a rail. Third place went to the other rider who went clear but did a very slow round.

'Second place, number twelve: Jade Lennox riding Onyx.' Jade grinned as she trotted back into the ring and over to the judge's truck. She was soon joined by Becca and Dusty.

'You've actually won the 1.10-metre class at Flaxton Sports!' Jade whispered to Becca as the ribbons were tied around their ponies' necks.

'And you got second!' Becca said. 'It's been a perfect day.'

As the winners cantered around the ring in a lap of honour, Jade was completely distracted from the prospect of having to leave her friends and her beautiful pony.

# Where is home?

The week leading up to Christmas was blissful. No school, perfect weather, and long lazy rides with Becca, Laura, Andy and Abby White, who was home from university.

'What do you study at university, Abby?' Laura asked, as they ambled along in the heavy sunshine.

'French, art history and philosophy,' Abby replied.

'What do you want to do when you've finished?' Laura asked. 'Do you want to be a teacher?'

Abby laughed. 'I haven't a clue yet, really. What do you want to be?'

'A vet,' Laura said decisively. 'I've known since I was four.'

'What about you guys?' Abby asked Jade and Becca.

'Maybe a wildlife photographer? Like for *National Geographic*,' Becca said quietly.

'Since when?' Laura cut in. 'I thought you wanted to be a vet too?'

Sensing the beginnings of an argument, Jade said, 'I'd like to work with horses, but not as a vet.'

'That's what I wanted to do when I was your age,' Abby said, sounding old. 'You'd probably have a way better chance of that than me, though, Jade — I hear you guys cleaned up at Flaxton. Come on, Brandy, get a move on.' Abby was riding Hamlet and leading her own horse which she'd lent to Laura.

There was only one dark cloud hanging over Jade, and that was the possibility of moving back to Auckland. It wasn't just the thought of the pain of abandoning Pip and leaving her friends that upset Jade, it was the worry of returning to her old school and Rose. Even just a week with Rose during the holidays had shown that they had both changed. Less than a year in Flaxton and Jade had become a country girl.

'Wake up, Jade!' Becca said, waving her hand in front of Jade's eyes.

'Sorry, I was miles away,' Jade said. 'What were you talking about?'

'Abby was telling us about the Pony Club Show-jumping Champs, and suggesting that we try out for the team next February.'

'Oh,' Jade said.

'You don't want to?' Becca asked, aghast.

'I do, but . . .' Jade paused, 'I may not be here in February.' Jade wasn't usually very good at keeping secrets, but somehow she hadn't been able to bring herself to tell Becca and Andy and Laura the bad news until now.

'What?' Laura said. 'Why?'

'Dad's not sure that he can get a job in Flaxton. And we've still got our old house in Auckland.'

'What will happen to Pip?' Becca asked, concerned.

'I don't know. I don't want to leave her, but I might have to. It's awful! Especially after all the help Mr White's given us. It's such a waste.' Jade couldn't help getting angry.

'I'll take her,' Becca said, seriously.

'Would you really?' Jade asked, relieved.

'We've got plenty of room on the farm, and she'd be no trouble.'

It seemed too easy to just give away her pony. Although Becca's offer took a weight off Jade's mind, it also made the move to Auckland seem more real.

'I don't want you to go,' Laura said tearfully, as the girls untacked the horses back at the Whites'.

'Believe me, I don't want to go either,' Jade said. 'I guess we just have to cross our fingers and hope Dad gets a job here.'

It was the day before Christmas Eve and, since his first night in Flaxton, Jade's dad hadn't mentioned the move back to Auckland again, and Jade was too scared to ask. She did her best to forget about it and tried to just enjoy having him around for Christmas.

'Are you going for a ride today?' her dad asked, as they ate breakfast together at the table.

'I was thinking of doing some Christmas shopping,' Jade said. 'It's going to be too hot for riding.' It was only eight-thirty and already there was a heat haze out on the road and the cicadas were whirring.

'Can I come with you? I need to do some shopping, too,' he said.

'Of course you can!' Jade said, hoping her dad might be able to give her some money. She loved buying presents, but hated asking for money from her granddad.

Her shopping list included horse mints for Pip, a calendar for Laura, a book and some chocolates for Mr and Mrs White, something horsey for Andy and Becca — and something, she didn't know what, for her dad and granddad.

It was a slow shopping trip, as her dad still wasn't allowed to drive. After walking to the shops, they were both hot and thirsty, so they stopped for a milkshake before attempting to find the items on Jade's list.

Their last stop was the saddlery, which was another half an hour's walk over the other side of town. There Jade found the mints for Pip, and, seeing that colourful, woven lead ropes were on special, she got one each for Becca and Andy. Walking up to the counter, she saw something else — the most beautiful black leather bridle. Pip's bridle, a hand-me-down from one of Abby's old ponies, was a touch too small. This one looked as though it would fit perfectly. Unfortunately, it was way beyond Jade's meagre budget.

'That's a good one, is it?' her dad asked, seeing Jade coveting the bridle. 'I'm so ignorant about all this equestrian stuff.'

'Yeah,' Jade said wistfully. 'It's a good one.'

'I still don't know what to get Granddad,' Jade said, sadly, as they walked home with the presents.

'To be honest, I'm struggling to think of anything, too,' her dad said. 'Terrible, aren't we?'

This conundrum was solved that evening when

Jade hopped on her bike and delivered the gifts, now wrapped in Christmas paper, to all of her friends. The last house she went to, Laura's, was looking very festive, with a big tree, lots of tinsel and a lovely smell of Christmas cake.

'Your house is so cosy,' Jade said, handing Laura the puppy calendar.

'Come through to the laundry,' Laura said. 'It's even cosier in here.'

Surprised, Jade followed. She soon saw what Laura meant, for in a corner of the laundry, next to the drier, lay Bubble, on a sheepskin rug in a basket, curled up with five perfect little black-and-white puppies.

'They're adorable!' Jade said, falling down to her knees to stroke the sleeping bundles.

'Would you like one?' Laura asked. 'Mum said that I wasn't allowed to give them to my friends as Christmas presents unless I asked first.'

'I shouldn't get one,' Jade said, thinking about Auckland. 'But I reckon my granddad would like one.'

'Yay!' Laura said. 'I love the puppies, but we

have to get rid of them. Bubble just keeps having them, don't you, dear?'

That night, Jade told her dad about the puppies. To her delight, he thought a puppy would make an excellent present and agreed to go to the pet shop the next day to buy the necessary accessories.

Coming home laden with a basket, a bag of puppy food, a chewy toy, a collar and a voucher for the puppy's shots, Jade's dad decided that a puppy was quite a lavish gift.

'Still, he's looked after you so well this year,' Jade's dad said, 'the old man deserves an impressive present.'

On Christmas morning, Jade got up at seven-thirty and walked to Laura's to collect the puppy. She chose a friendly little bitch with a speckled stomach and deep brown eyes.

Laura's mum had put the puppy in a cardboard box, but on the way home Jade abandoned the box and cuddled the puppy to her chest. The puppy kept licking Jade's hands and nipping with sharp little milk-teeth.

When Jade got home, her dad distracted her granddad in the kitchen with the ham while she arranged the puppy sweetly in the basket, under their Christmas tree. The secret didn't last long, though. As soon as Jade left the puppy in the living room and went to the kitchen, the puppy started whining and yapping.

'What the devil?' her granddad said. 'Is there a dog under the tree?'

Jade and her father laughed. 'Merry Christmas!' Jade said to her granddad. 'You'd better come through and see your present before it wets the basket.'

'Too late,' Granddad said, kneeling slowly and picking up the slightly damp puppy.

'Well, hello, missy,' he said, trying not to sound too enchanted. 'Are you for me?'

When Jade came back with an old towel to put in the puppy's basket, she found her granddad sitting on the couch, cuddling his present.

'What are you going to call her?' Jade said,

scratching the pup behind its ears.

'It's a bit unoriginal,' Granddad said, 'but how about Holly? It being Christmas and all.'

'Holly's a lovely name!' Jade said.

When Jade's dad returned from the kitchen, convinced that the ham was at the right temperature, they opened the rest of the presents.

'I'm sorry it's so boring,' Jade said, passing her dad a book-shaped parcel. 'It's more for me really, too.'

Her dad laughed. 'You didn't need to get me anything. I'm just happy that we're back together, and that you've done so well this year. I'm proud of you.' He tore the paper off the book and laughed again. It was *Showjumping* by Michaela Lewis.

'This is good,' her dad said slowly, opening the cover and examining the Contents page. 'It'll give me some inside knowledge. When I'm next at a horse show, I'll know what to say.'

Jade thought sadly that her dad might never have to go to a horse show again.

'This one's for you, Jade,' her granddad said. 'From me and your father.'

It was a strange, lumpy gift. Jade tore off the paper quickly and found the beautiful black bridle that she'd seen at the saddlery. She gasped. 'Thank you! This is absolutely perfect! But, if we're leaving, when will I get to use it?'

'That's the second half of the present,' her dad said. 'I probably shouldn't have kept it as a surprise until now, but I wanted to be sure I had the job before I told you.'

'Are we staying?' Jade asked, with shining eyes.

'Looks like it. I start my job at the *Flaxton Times* in the New Year. A reporter who can't drive isn't much use, but luckily they were in need of an editor.'

Jade threw herself across the room and gave her dad an enormous bear hug. 'Thank you, thank you, thank you!' she said, kissing his cheek.

'It's going to be quite a change of scene from the *Herald*,' her dad said. 'But that's what I need, I think: a change of scene. Flaxton seems to have done wonders for you, young lady. Perhaps I should get a horse, too?' They all laughed.

'Yes, and Mr White can teach you to ride,' Jade

said, giggling hysterically.

The last present under the tree was the little bag of mints for Pip.

'The ham's still got a couple of hours until it's ready,' Granddad said. 'Why don't we take Holly for a ride in the car and give Pip her present?'

'Yes, let's!' Jade said, over the moon. Now that she knew they'd be staying in Flaxton, the day was perfect.

'This isn't the way to the Whites',' Jade told her granddad from the back seat of the Falcon. 'Where are we going?'

'Just a little tiki tour,' Granddad said.

'Dad, do you know where we're going?' Jade asked. 'What about you, Holly?' she said, addressing the warm, squirmy bundle in her lap. 'Are you behind this?'

'It was supposed to be another surprise, but if you're going to ask questions all the way then I may as well tell you,' Jade's dad said in mock frustration. 'I've bought us a house.'

'What?' Jade squealed. 'Already?' Her granddad parked outside an old strawberry-pink bungalow. 'Is this it?'

'I'm afraid so. Shocking colour, eh?'

'Terrible,' Jade agreed, leaping out of the car.

However, the colour turned out to be the house's only real fault. There was a good-sized back yard, with a lawn and fruit trees — two lemons, a walnut and a saggy old Granny Smith. Inside there was a big room at the front for her dad, a smaller room overlooking the garden for Jade, and a spare room for visitors.

'Thank you, Dad. I love it,' Jade said, hugging her father.

'Sorry there isn't a paddock for Pip,' he said. 'Hopefully Mr White won't mind her staying a bit longer. Now that I've got some cash from selling our old house, we can at least pay for grazing.'

While Granddad, Holly and Jade wished the horses a Merry Christmas, Jade's dad went to find Mr White. Predictably, Mr White was reluctant to accept the cheque that Jade's dad gave him.

'This really isn't necessary,' Mr White protested weakly.

'Please, I insist. I'd like to buy Pip from you, for Jade.'

'But this is much more than I paid for her.'

'It's only a fraction of what I owe you for being so generous and caring to Jade over the past year. I'm not hearing another word about it. And expect regular payments for grazing from now on. I don't want Jade to feel like a charity case.'

When Jade's dad had finally won this polite argument, and when Hamlet had finished stealing Pip's horse mints, Mrs White invited everyone in for a quick slice of Christmas cake and a glass of bubbly and orange juice (mostly orange juice for Jade).

'Cheers to a new start in Flaxton,' Jade's dad said, raising his glass. 'And cheers to Jim and Ellen for their kindness.'

They'd been sitting on the Whites' deck for nearly an hour, soaking up the sun, chatting about Jade and her dad's new house and being charmed by Holly, when Granddad swore loudly.

'Language, Dad!' Jade's father said, teasingly. 'What's wrong?'

'The ham! It'll be burnt to a crisp.'

Jade scooped up the puppy and hurried out to the Falcon.

'If it's completely ruined, come back here for dinner — we have plenty of food,' Abby called, grinning.

'It'll be fine,' Jade replied. 'But, if it's OK, I'll be around tomorrow for a ride.'

'Of course,' Mr White said. 'I'd expect nothing else from you.'

# Four ways to make friends with a pony

**1** If you approach a pony quietly, slowly and towards its head, it is more likely to be pleased to see you. If you run up behind a pony, laughing and shouting, it will be frightened and either shy away or kick with its strong hind legs. Just think how startling it would be if an equine friend came galloping up behind you.

Only approach a pony if its owner doesn't mind. If you see a lovely chestnut mare in a paddock and want to say hello, just call to it from over the fence.

**2** Even if they don't understand every word you say, ponies love a good conversation.

As you approach a pony, or call to it from the fence, say its name in a kind, confident voice. If you don't know the pony's name, clicking your tongue is a good way to get its attention. Sometimes, if you make a snickering noise (by rolling your lips as if you were blowing a raspberry), a pony will mimic you and snicker back. This is a good sign that you and the pony are becoming friends.

When you have a pony's attention, and are patting, leading, grooming or feeding it, keep the conversation going. Praise the pony if it is behaving well, ask how its day has been going, and keep it informed. For example: 'Hello, Pip! How are you, today? Nice and sunny, isn't it? Have you been rolling? Your rump is all dusty. OK, I'm just going to put your halter on now. Good girl!'

(3) Generally, ponies love being patted and groomed. When you're patting a pony, stroke

firmly in the direction that its coat grows. If you pat too gently, the pony might think that your hand is a fly and its skin will shiver. To stop flies annoying them, ponies often stamp their hooves. When you are near a pony, it is a very good idea to wear covered shoes.

Most ponies enjoy a good scratch on the forehead or eyebrow, but some would rather you didn't touch their face. If your equine friend is head-shy, stick to patting its neck.

4 Offering a treat is a good way to make friends with a pony. A ripe apple or carrot will be well received. (If the pony has a small mouth, these might need to be broken in half.) Horse mints are a favourite too, or even just a handful of lush grass or clover. When feeding a pony, remember to keep the palm of your hand as flat as possible. That way, when the pony bites the apple it won't accidentally take your fingers off.

If the pony isn't yours, it is a good idea to ask the owner before feeding it a treat, just in case it's on a diet. If you've called a pony in a paddock over to the fence, a small handful of grass or clover shouldn't do any harm. Just be careful not to feed it anything poisonous. If you don't recognize a plant, don't feed it to a pony.

If you are eating your lunch near a pony, you might find that it is very interested in your honey sandwiches, packet of chips, or chocolate biscuits. Like people, ponies love sugary and salty foods. While these are OK as an occasional treat, an apple or carrot is much healthier.